GHOSTSLAYER

Parl Dro tore up the plank and his fingers thrust through the soft rot beneath and touched the single bone embedded there. It had belonged to the ghost, when the ghost had been a man. Through the concrete essence of that bone, the ghost, unwilling to depart, had kept its hideous link with the condition of life. A hundred persons had since died because of it. It had exulted in their screams of terror and agony. It would have killed the rest of the world if it could.

Even as Dro raised the bone toward the jaws of his vise, the ghost was on him. Made corporeal by its long pesudo-existence, it had the energy to drag him down and fling him over.

The dead who lived, like the mirror image, right hand in reverse, tended to attack leftward or sinister. It occurred to Dro quite abruptly that **the ghost had fastened its teeth and nails into the calf of his left leg, ripping and gnawing at him. . . .**

KILL
THE
DEAD

Tanith Lee

DAW Books, Inc.
Donald A. Wollheim, Publisher

1633 Broadway, New York, N.Y. 10019

FIRST PRINTING, SEPTEMBER 1980

1 2 3 4 5 6 7 8 9

DAW TRADEMARK REGISTERED
U.S. PAT. OFF. MARCA
REGISTRADA. HECHO EN U.S.A.

PRINTED IN U.S.A.

TABLE OF CONTENTS

Dedication:

To VALENTINE

CHAPTER ONE

———••◦━◉━◦••———

"Cilny—we are in danger."

The shadows did not answer.

The only way down from the mountain was by a steep, tortuous steel-blue road. About ten miles below the pass the road leveled grudgingly and curled itself around toward an upland valley where trees and a village were growing together. Half a mile before it reached the village, it swerved by the wall of a curious leaning house.

There were trees growing by the house, too. Their roots had gone in under the foundations, seeking the water course that was otherwise evident in the stone well just inside the ironwork gate. Gradually, the roots of the trees were levering the house over. Extravagant cracks ran up the walls, and a dark-green climbing plant had fastened on these. Over on the north side, however, the house itself had at some time put out a strong supporting growth: a three-story stone tower.

The tower was probably defensive in origin. Its three narrow windows looked northwest toward the mountain, over the smoky tops of the trees.

The sun was down. At this hour the mountain seemed to take on exactly the twilight color of the sky behind it, and might almost have been made of a slightly swarthy and imperfect glass. Modestly, other more distant heights had retreated into soft charcoal strokes sketched over the horizon.

From the uppermost window of the tower, it was possible to see the mountain road very clearly, even in the dusk. And better still after stars, as if ignited by tapers, burst into white dots of brilliance overhead, and a pale quarter moon floated up in the east.

A figure was coming down the road from the pass. It was wrapped up in a black hooded mantle, but its general shape and mode of walking showed it to be masculine. Showed, too, that it was lame. At each stride, for strides they still were, there came a measured hesitation on the left side.

When the black-mantled lame man striding down the road was some seventy paces from the house, the girl at the tower window drew back swiftly into the room. Turning to the shadows there, she repeated her whisper with a restrained desperation.

"Cilny—we're in danger—terrible danger. Can you hear me? Are you there? Oh Cilny, answer me."

This time there was a response. The shadows, at their very thickest in one of the tower's deep corners, seemed to part. Pale as the quarter moon, a shape slipped from between them.

"I'm here," said a voice less a whisper than the rustle of a leaf on one of the trees outside. "What is it?"

"Darling Cilny, my only and best sister," said the girl who had watched at the window, "there's a man walking along the road. He's lame in the left leg, and dressed in black. I may be mistaken, but I think I know him."

The pale moon shadow laughed gently, a leaf laughing.

"When did you ever meet such a man, Ciddey?"

"Not meet. Never met. Never *to* meet, I hope and I pray. But I've heard talk of such a man. Old tales."

"What a mystery. Won't you tell me?"

"If it's he—his name is Parl Dro. But he has another name. A trade name. *Ghost-Killer*."

The pale moon shadow, who was also a girl, long-haired and slender like the first, but—unlike the first—oddly transparent, drew back a little way, and her translucent hand drifted to her translucent mouth.

"We don't want such a person here," she whispered in her leaf voice.

"No. We don't. So, hide, Cilny. *Hide.*"

Parl Dro had been looking at the house steadily, with two raven-black eyes, as he came down the road. Mostly because such a dwelling betokened the proximity of the village he was aiming to reach before full night set in. Not that he was un-used to sleeping on bare ground. He was as accustomed to that as he was to the relentless grinding ache of the lame leg. He had known that hurt, in any case, some years, and had carefully taught himself that familiarity, even with pain, bred contempt. There had also been trouble not far behind him, which he did not want to dwell on, because probably there would be more trouble not far ahead.

It had periodically happened that, arriving in some rural, out-of-the-way place, Parl Dro, limping long-leggedly in his swathing of black, had been mistaken for Death. Card-casting and similar divination generally foretold his arrival in the shape of the ominous King of Swords. But then, his calling being what it was, that was not so inappropriate.

He had been subconsciously aware for half an hour or so of scrutiny from the house, and had not bothered with it. It was not unlikely that a stranger would be stared at out in the wilds. Then, when he had followed the curve of the road and come level with the antique ironwork gate, something prompted him to stop. It might have been that uncanny seventh sense of his that had made him what he was. Or it might have been only that more usual and more common sixth sense, the inner antenna that responded to quite human auras of trouble or mystique. He could not, at this stage, be sure. The house itself, leaning and overgrown in the gathering of night, was so suggestive of the bizarre, he was inclined to dismiss his sudden awareness as imagination only. But Dro was not one to brush aside any occurrence too lightly, even his own rare fancies.

Presently, he pushed open the iron gate and went into the paved yard.

Over a well craned a dead fig tree. The other trees, jealous of its nearness to the water source, had sucked the life out of it. Truly, a malevolent notion. The house door, deep in a

stone porch, was of wood, old and very warped. He went to
the door and struck it a couple of times.

As he waited, the bright stars intensified against the night,
and the ghostly moon, in the way of ghosts, solidified and
assumed reality.

A beetle ran up the ivy plant along the wall.

Nobody had answered the knock, though somebody was
here for sure. The whole house seemed to be listening now,
holding its breath. Peering over at him. Possibly the occupant
of the house, alone after sunset, was quite properly chary of
opening the door to unknown travelers.

Dro's methods did not include unnecessarily terrorizing the
innocent—though he was quite capable of it if the occasion
warranted. He stepped back and moved away from the old
door.

The yard was now hung with curtains of dark shadow. Yet
starglow pierced the trees and glimmered in the well water.
. . . There was something about the well. Something.

Parl Dro moved across to it. He stood and looked over the
rim and beheld his own faceless silhouette blocking out the
luminous darkness of the sky. A rusty chain went down into
the water. He let the impulse order him, and began to wind
the chain up by its handle. The chain dragged from the
bucket at its other end, and the handle creaked sourly in the
quiet. His seventh sense was very definitely operating now.
The bucket slapped free of the well at the same instant the
house door crashed open.

There was no preliminary warning, no stir in the house
that had been audible outside. One second the pool of the
night lay undisturbed, the next second broken by the opened
door, the dash of thin bright light thrown out across the yard
from her pallid lamp.

He got the impression altogether of great pallor from the
girl who stood there, a pallor that for an instant sent the
familiar dazzle up his spine. But it was not quite that pallor
after all. It was the bleached dress, the flaxen hair in five slim
braids, three down her back, one each side of her face and
looped over her ears. That, and her white skin, white hands,
the right holding the narrow flame in its tube of greenish
glass, the left holding the long, bared, white-shining knife.

Dro had halted the bucket, his hand still taut on the
handle. He stayed like that, and watched her. He might have

expected the not unnatural interrogation and bluff: Who are you? How dare you? My man will soon be here and see to you. None of that came. The girl simply yelled at him, in a shrill voice: "Get out! Go away!"

He paused a moment, letting her words hang. Then he said, pitching his own voice to carry level and clear, "Can't I draw a drink of water from your well, first? I did knock. I thought there was no one home."

He had a beautiful voice, marvelous diction that often worked like a charm on people, particularly women. Not on this one.

"Get out, I said. Now!"

He paused again, then let the handle go abruptly. The chain unwound with a screech and the bucket plummeted under. He did it to startle her, and so it did. The seventh sense was alert as a nerve, bristling. He walked around the well and back toward the door, toward her. He wanted to be sure, and that meant eliminating other explanations for her unfriendliness. As he went, he slipped the hood off his head. As he walked slowly, his lameness was minimized, and he was graceful. He kept his hands loose, free of the mantle, showing he had no weapon ready or considered.

Parl Dro was a remarkable looking man. Not as young, maybe, as he had been ten years before, but with an extraordinary handsomeness that had laid a velvety somber bloom across a concert of strong features. Lips and nose, cheekbones and jaw were those of some legendary emperor on a coin. The eyes, with their fabulous impenetrable blackness, were an exact match with the long straight black fringes of hair. Characteristics, both physical and immaterial, hinted a zodiacal latitude somewhere between the earth sign of the bull and the fire sign of the serpent.

As he strolled into the light of the small lamp, the girl must see all this. See, too, the slightly cold and acid twist to the mouth that dismissed sexual immoderation and therefore threat of it, the invisible yet quite precisely ruled line that seemed to link the balance of both eyes—a mark of calculation, intelligence and control above and beyond the normal. Only a fool would judge this man robber, rapist or similar practitioner. And the girl did not seem to be a fool. Yet she was afraid, and menacing. And remained so.

As suddenly as she had thrown open the door, she slashed out with the knife in her hand.

Parl Dro stepped back, a sloping lame man's step, but perfectly timed, and the blade carved the air an inch from his side. He was somewhat above average height, and the girl not tall. She had been aiming as close to his heart as she could.

"Now will you take yourself off!" she cried, in a panic apparently at her own intentions as much as the missed stroke. "You're not welcome."

"Obviously."

He stood beyond her range, continuing to look at her.

"What do you *want*?" she spat at last.

"I told you. A drink of water."

"You don't want water."

"How odd. I thought I did. Thank you for putting me right."

She blinked. Her long lashes were almost gray, her eyes a hot, dry cindery color, nearly green, not quite.

"Don't try word games with me. Just go. Or I'll call the dogs."

"You mean those dogs I've heard snarling and barking ever since I came through the gate."

At that, she flung the knife right at him. It was a wide cast, after all; he judged as much and let it come by. It brushed his sleeve and clattered against the side of the well. He had had much worse to deal with a few days back.

"Too bad," he said. "You should practice more."

He turned and walked off and left her poised there, staring. At the gate he hesitated and glanced around. She had not moved. She would be shocked, but also dreaming that she had got rid of him. It was too soon for that.

"Perhaps," he called, "I'll see you tomorrow."

Leaving her knife lying by the well, she flashed back into the house and slammed the door. In the stillness, he heard the sound of bolts.

He pulled the hood over his head.

His face was grim and meditative as he turned again onto the road and started toward the village.

The village was like a hundred others. One broad central street which branched straight off the road. The central street had a central water-course, a stream, natural or connived, that carried off the sewage, and in which strange phosphorescent fish swam by night. Stepping stones crossed the water at intervals, and at other intervals alleys as narrow as needles ran between the houses. Most of the buildings facing on the main thoroughfare were shops, their open fronts nocturnally fenced in by locked gates. Houses on the thoroughfare had blind walls, keeping their windows to the rear, save for the rare slit that dropped a slender bar of yellow gold onto the ground.

The three inns, however, made up in light and noise what the village, mute and dark amid its grain fields and orchards and the vineyard scent of late summer, otherwise lacked.

The first inn Dro bypassed. It was too loud and largely too active for his requirements. The second inn was but two doors away, and plainly served also as the village brothel. There had been enough trouble with women. As he went by, a sly-eyed curly girl shouted from the open entrance the immemorial invitation, and, when he ignored her, screamed an insult connecting virility, or lack of it, to a limp. That made him smile a moment. The final inn stood on a corner formed by the central street and an adjacent alley. It too was loud and bright, but to a lesser degree. He found the writing on the sign was virtually illegible. The door was also shut, as if to say: *I am not actually inviting any of you to enter.*

When Dro pushed the door wide enough to be admitted, the entire roomful of occupants turned to see who was coming in. Their reaction on learning was disturbed, but vague.

Parl Dro's fame, or perhaps *infamy*, tended to precede him. It was quite probable some here would surmise his identity. It seemed likely the girl in the leaning house had done so. But if the diners and drinkers of this inn divined who had come among them, they were not eager, or had no reason, to act upon it. Even the singing, which was concentrated at the far end of the room, about the hearth and its cumbersomely turning spits, had not faltered.

Dro let the door reel shut behind him. He stood a few extra seconds, allowing more determined gawpers to satisfy themselves. Then he walked, slow and scarcely lame, quietly to one of the long tables. As he seated himself, the slightest, softest, most involuntary of sighs escaped him as the turmoil in the crippled leg subsided to mere pain.

The others seated at the table shifted, like grass touched by

a breeze, and resettled. They eyed each other over their cups
and bowls, the bones they were chewing, the cards or dice or
riddle-blocks they were gaming with. An older looking boy in
a leather apron came up, a meat knife through his belt, a
bottle and cup in his hand.

"What'll you have?"

"Whatever there is."

"There's this," said the boy. He dumped the cup on the
table and poured a rough glycerine alcohol into it from the
bottle. "And that," he added, pointing to the spits, the stew
pot, the shelves of hot loaves and baking onions stacked over
them.

"Don't waste your time," said one of the gamesters at the
table. "*He* doesn't eat." He picked up and showed the card he
had just dealt. It was the King of Swords, its four black
points painted on like thorns, the hooded high-crowned mon-
arch brooding between them. The death card, Bad Luck.

"He means," explained the older boy, "you look like
Death."

"I certainly feel like it," said Dro. He pushed off his hood,
picked up the cup and drained it. "The third of a loaf," he
elaborated to the boy, "and a couple of slices of that sheep
you're burning over the fire."

"We always burn the sheep here," said the boy wittily, "to
be sure they're properly dead before you eat them."

"I'm relieved you take the same precautions with the
bread."

Somebody laughed. Somebody else mimed a man trying to
acquire a bite out of a live loaf. The boy filled Dro's cup
again and went off to the hearth, shouldering his way, mur-
derously flourishing the meat knife, through the singers. As
some of the raucous chorus broke off, Dro caught a couple
of bars of perfect music, sheer and fine as a shining fish
glancing through river mud. The sources of the music were
firstly strings, turned high as clouds, then suddenly also a
pipe tuned even higher. Dro partly inclined his head, waiting
for the next exquisite bar, but the howling song started up
again and the music submerged in it.

The boy was back and slapped down a platter.

"Stick this fork in it. If it goes *baaa*, I'll put it back on the
spit for a while."

Dro pierced the mutton with the fork and a dozen voices bleated along the length of the table.

"Better fetch the shepherd," said Dro, "before the wolf gets his flock." He began to eat, economically. A little silence gathered.

Eventually someone said:

"It'd be a lame wolf, wouldn't it?"

A neighbor jogged his elbow. "Shut up, idiot. I recognize who he is now."

"Yes," said another. "And I do, too. I thought he was a legend."

Dro went on economically eating. One of the men said to him: "We've guessed who you are."

Dro sat back and smiled enigmatically at no one.

"Am I to be the last to know?"

They shuffled. Somebody said, as somebody always said, "Don't think I want to share this table with you."

But none of them moved away. Indeed, one or two more were edging over from other parts of the room, drawn as if to the scene of a lurid crime. Dro went on eating and drinking, slow, and oddly isolated from the whirlpool he was creating. He was as used to this as to rough ground, as to the pain that walked with him. Used to it, and able now and then to use it in turn.

The remarks came gently, cautiously, laying ripples of emotion over the warm air.

"What do you think of yourself, doing what you do?"

"How do you sleep nights?"

"He sleeps all right. There'll be plenty with cause to thank him."

"And plenty who won't thank him."

"Plenty who curse him, eh, Ghost-Killer? How many curses fly down the roads with you? Is that what keeps you looking young?"

"You were lamed by a malediction, isn't that so?"

"No. Not that way. One of his victims stuck a claw in him at the gate out. He hasn't aged since then."

All around the spinning currents of these unanswered sallies, the room grew quieter and quieter. Dro heard the singing fade out, but the music went out too. He did not look about, just waited for the cue that must inevitably come. He finished what he wanted of his meal, and was drinking the last stinging mouthful from his cup when the cue dropped into the pool.

"Well, you've had a wasted journey to this place, Parl Dro. We haven't any deadalive here."

"Oh, but you're wrong," he said, and they jumped at his immaculate voice which had been silent such a while. "Half a mile back along the road. The leaning house with the stone tower."

He could have portioned the silence with the boy's meat knife after he said that. It was not exactly that they knew and had been withholding it from him, more that they had suspected, and the confirmation chilled them. Of course, there was no need to tell them it had been another place he was making for altogether, that this was an unscheduled task.

The first of the men who had baa-ed, said very low, "He means the Soban house."

Another of the men added, "That's Ciddey's house. There's nothing there. Except poverty, a little kiss of madness."

The boy in the leather apron was at Dro's shoulder, leaning to refill Dro's cup. Dro put his hand over the cup. The boy poured words instead.

"The Sobans were the masters here five years ago. Old Soban and his two daughters. But they lost their money and the village bought the land."

"They lost their money because the father drank it. He was drinking it before Ciddey was old enough to bite."

"Then he'd sell things," said the first man. "Botched-up rubbish—ridiculous stuff."

"There was a wonderful thing, supposed to come from some foreign place, wasn't there? And it was just a couple of old scythes welded together. He'd get the smith to help him, Soban would. The carpenter, the mason. Everyone—"

"Someone told me," said another of the men, "he sold Ciddey's baby teeth as a charm necklace."

"That's crazy."

"Ciddey's crazy too. Pity, because she's nice-looking enough. We leave her to herself, for old time's sake. She lives alone in that house."

"Not quite alone," said Dro.

"The father drank himself into the graveyard years before," the first man said. "Do you mean him?"

"I don't think so."

"There was a story," said the first man. "The girls played about with herbs. Witch charms, poisons maybe. They got sick of the father drinking and . . . saw to him."

"And that's a lie," said someone.

Dro was aware of the singing group detaching itself from the hearth and swarming over. The minstrel who had played the exquisite music was beginning to appear in fragments, now a threadbare red sleeve, now a dirty green sleeve, now a dark gold head and a long nose, between the shoulders and gesticulations of the crowd.

They were excited, and nervous. An event was happening in the midst of uneventfulness. The musician, staying clear, carefully keeping his head down over retuning the peculiar instrument beside the spits, showed a desire to remain uninvolved, and thereby a derivation not of this village.

"There was the second daughter," someone said finally, just behind Dro's left ear.

"Ciddey's sister? Nothing funny there."

"Yes, there was. Didn't Cilny Soban run off and drown herself in the stream the north side of the mountain? Not exactly what I'd call normal."

"It's true, Parl Dro," the elderly boy said. "Two herders found her in the morning when they were taking the cows up to graze."

"Cilny was lying at the bottom of the stream, she was," said the first man dolefully, "but the water's so clear in the spring you could see straight through. One of the boys is a bit simple. He thought she was a water spirit, lying there in her nightgown, with a wreath of flowers on her head and fish swimming about in her hair."

"What do you think of that, eh, Parl Ghost-Killer?"

Dro removed his hand from the cup and let the boy fill it again. The crowd had got itself well into the informative stage, anxious to elicit a response from him. They had commenced pressing rumor and snippets of memory on him like gifts, waiting for him to crow. But the King of Swords merely sat and brooded, letting them heap the platter.

They were putting great emphasis on the stresses of the girls' two names, telling him now how *Sidd-dayy* and *Sill-nee* had been, loving and near one hour, at each other's throats the next. Once or twice, one sister might look at a village man, and then the other sister would go wild, shrieking that such a wooing, let alone marriage, was beneath the Soban blood. When Cilny had made away with herself the previous spring, nobody had dropped down in a fit of surprise. When Ciddey demanded the corpse be burned not buried and the ashes delivered to her in a stone pot, not even the priest had had much to say. The Sobans had always been a pagan tribe, amoral and unstable. Since the death of Cilny, Ciddey was rarely seen. Sometimes someone might spot her by night, walking along the slopes below the mountain, or up in the tower window, staring out. In her pig-headed way, just like her father, she expected the village to put food and other essentials at her gate, free of charge, its tithe to her house. With a self-deprecating amused grimace, between shame and pride, the village admitted that it did so. Nobody had actually considered whether drowned Cilny might come back to haunt. But now that they did consider, they would not be amazed if she had.

Dro sipped from the third cup.

The stream-death might explain the ambience at the well, the pulse of supernatural force linked to water. The pot of cremated ashes was significant. It was coming time to reward the crowd with a reaction, and then to damp their fire. As he sat, picturing the flower-wreathed water maiden stretched under the glassy stream, he became aware that the musician had moved from the hearth, and was after all stealing closer. He slid through and into the crowd with a very practiced ease, attracting small notice. Intrigued but not astonished, Dro kept still.

"What do you say, Parl Dro?" the boy in the apron asked.

"I say there's a ghost at the leaning house," Dro said, virtually what he had said at the start, but a little eddy of satisfaction drifted up. The musician, instrument across his back now, was filtering through the throng like a curl of color-stained steam.

"What'll you do?"

"Oh, I think I'll go to bed. That is if you have a room here I can use."

Confounded, the crowd muttered. They had expected him to leap at once out through the door again, no doubt.

"But aren't you going to call on Ciddey Soban?"

"Apparently not," he told them. He rose, paying no heed to the blazing chord that was struck in his crippled leg. The musician had halted, about a foot away, molded exactly between two burly laborers, just as if he had grown there from a tiny seed planted in the floor. He was only an inch or two shorter than Dro, but lightly built as a reed.

Dro regarded the boy in the apron.

"The room?"

"I'll show you. What about Cilny deadalive?"

"What about her?"

There were angry murmurs now. As he began to walk through, Dro felt the new hardening and congealing of the press around the table, not wanting to let him go this casually after he had worked them to such a pitch. Even in the thick of that, however, Dro was entirely conscious of the featherweight grip that delicately flickered out the coin bag from the inner pocket of his mantle. Dro did not glance the musician's way. A pickpocket's skill was not one he necessarily despised, nor did he necessarily grudge its reward.

The boy led Dro to the stair.

"Straight up. Door to the left. Aren't you going to do *anything* about Cilny? You're supposed to be a legend."

The crowd surged sulkily, not looking at Dro, like a woman who thought herself slighted. The musician was tuning the instrument again, leaning on a table, engrossed, dull gold hair falling in his eyes, innocent.

The older boy assumed a sneer as he watched Dro begin the lame man's crow-like hopping up the stair.

"Well, what a disappointment you turned out to be."

Dro paused on the landing and turned on the boy the most dazzling and friendly smile he was ever likely to have received. The Ghost-Killer seemed to be waiting again. Unnerved, the boy jeered: "A real disappointment. I hope I never have to see a worse one."

"Keep away from mirrors," said Dro, "and you won't."

He stepped through the left-hand sinister door.

CHAPTER TWO

An hour before dawn, Parl Dro was on a narrow wooden bridge above a savage river. Swollen by melted upland snow, the water crashed about the piled stone pylons of the bridge, snapping its jaws hungrily at those who passed over. But there was something on the bridge that was worse than the river. It had been a man once. Now it was a fleshless, long-nailed shape, solidified by years of post-mortem manifestation, capable of appearing solid and real as the river below. More real, actually, than the bridge, whose timbers were in parts rotted away. Hate had kept it there, a hatred of all who remained alive after it had died.

There had been a conflict of wills since moonrise, a battle that had kept the ghost to one end of the bridge, Parl Dro at the other. Only very gradually had each been able to beat a way through the other's aphysical defenses. Only very gradually had each been able to draw nearer to the other and thus to the ultimate fight which would decide between them. Dro was certain that the psychic link was to be found somewhere at the center of the bridge, the spot at which the ghost generally laid hold of those who came there, biting at them with its long teeth from which the gums had shriveled away, clawing the organs out of their bodies. For hours, since moonrise, Parl Dro had been wrenching his way toward that area, while trying simultaneously to hold the ghost off from it. The ghost roared and sizzled its rage and sick hurt as it fought him. The man, drenched in sweat and psychosomatically bruised as if from a physical beating, fought back. It had been like climbing a vertical precipice while in the crisis of an unremitting fever. Now, he was a mere three inches from the tilted plank where he had reasoned the link must be.

To summon the final strength to rip the plank away and come at that link, brought a new dimension of horror and strain, which sent a whirling piercing nausea through him, body and soul. Nevertheless, he felt his hand grab hold of the wood, the muscles of arm and shoulder activated as if by remote and magical control. He tore up the plank, and his fingers thrust through the soft rot beneath and touched the single bone embedded there. It had belonged to the ghost, when the ghost had been a man, mislaid on the bridge when the ghost had violently died there. Through the concrete essence of that bone, the ghost, unwilling to depart, had kept its hideous link with the condition of life. A hundred persons had since died because of it. It had exulted in their screams of terror and agony. It would have killed the rest of the world if it could. Now it was as approximate to extinction, or at least to metamorphosis, as Parl Dro's two hands were approximate to each other. For one hand now held the bone, and the other the small but lethal vise which would crush that bone into a thousand meaningless splinters.

But in those instants, when all Dro's considerable powers had been focused on securing the link, the deadalive thing had found the space to win through.

Even as Dro raised the bone toward the jaws of the vise, the ghost was on him. Made corporeal by its long pseudo-existence, it had the energy to drag him down and to fling him over.

Dro heard the clamor of shattered timbers far off, at the same time as thunder passed through his skull. He realized dimly, as a storm of water spat in his eyes, that the ghost had smashed him bodily through the rotten struts of the bridge. Now he hung upside down, but still miraculously caught by knees and calves in the wood above. His body rocked against one of the stony pylons from the gush of the river, which every fourth breath or so went over his head, blinding him and causing him to swallow its fluid. He somehow had not lost the bone, for he could feel it embedded in his hand, but the vise was gone; he had let go of it in the shock of falling.

It seemed a year, but it was less than a minute before he came to understand the brittle texture of the bone, the hard surface of the pylon against which the river was ramming him over and over again. His head was full of choked water, his very brain seemed full of it, and the drumming of his own blood. He swung like a dead crow from a post, into and out of pain, unconsciousness and drowning, but he still remembered enough to start to hammer the brittle psychic bone against the stone of the pylon.

Ridiculously, stunned, he had forgotten about the creature he was fighting. When the blade of a new torture went through his left leg, he stupidly wondered if it was broken.

The dead who lived, like the mirror image, right hand in reverse, tended to attack leftward or sinister. Which made the hearts of men very vulnerable to them. It occurred to Dro quite abruptly that the ghost had fastened its teeth and nails into the calf of his left leg, ripping and gnawing at him.

Knowledge of the true facts of the pain made it unbearable. He began to utter strange long-drawn hoarse hymns of agony. Through these, the ghost kept up its labor upon his flesh, and he, mindless and screaming, clubbed the bone again and again into the stones of the pylon, his hand with it, till both were gaudy with blood.

The bone splintered suddenly, but the agony in his leg did not go away. He thought the ghoul still gnawed on him long after he had destroyed it. And long after the men had carried him away from the bridge, with a white sun scalding in his eyes, he thought so.

And quite often, as now, he would think so again, living through the sequence in the precise recurring format of a dream.

At one time it would have taken him an hour or more, sweating and shivering, to recover from this dream. Now recovery was swift. A minute: less. The only curious result was an impulse to reach down and touch his calf, as if to make sure it was still attached to him. But that was quickly over. Familiarity again. Contempt again. In any case, the crack of window showed a pale blue lake lying placidly in the middle of the village, between the eastern roofs, which was not a lake but the initiation of sunrise.

Nothing and no one but he seemed to be stirring at the inn. He utilized what facilities it had to offer, including the flat, iron-tasting water tapped from a cask in the room below, and another piece of burned loaf. He had left a handful of money, enough to cover his account generously, lying on the mattress where the ghoul had gnawed him in his sleep. Dro was no shorter of cash than he had anticipated. What the minstrel-thief had stolen from him with such artistry was a bag of smooth pebble clinkers. Nor would he be the first pickpocket to be edified by such a haul from Parl Dro's ill-omened black mantle.

Outside, a scatter of birds were whistling and piping to entice the sun. The lake had mounted higher and overtopped the roofs without spilling. A water rose was unfolding in the bottom of it.

Dro walked up the main street toward the steel-blue road. At one point, where an alley ran off into a yard with a public well, some women were gossiping in hushed voices over their buckets. He meant to be seen, and they saw him, and pointed him out needlessly to each other. A young one, with lily skin, stared at him, then blushed and looked away.

He was glad to have been noticed. It would save him the business of advertising his departure in any other manner.

The lily girl, pursuing him at a safe distance, even beheld him take the curve of the road which led eastward away from the village, and, more importantly, from the house with the tower.

Presently the road climbed up into some low hills. Beyond lay a rolling map of long, softly pleated lands, tending first through dove pastels and then startling greens as the sun winged higher up the sky; eventually into the dream-like blue masks of distance. That was the route he had been going, would be going on to. But not just yet. Not now.

He sat on a slope where a colonnade of trees stalked, like furled plumes, back toward the upland valley and the village. The trees gave color, shade and a pleasant noise of air swimming through leaves. He could see the village, quite small but very clear, below him. Also the switch of the road, leading around the old house and up the mountain, which was a smooth marble cone by day.

As the morning matured, Dro saw the village come fully alive. Miniature figures filled the street, little toy animals were herded out to pasture. When the warm breeze blew the right way, he could hear cows lowing, sheep which sounded more like cats, dogs barking, a hammer striking on metal, the wheels of a cart.

A short while before noon, a party of men and women went along the street, onto the road, and walked to the house with the tower. They stood about there for some minutes. When the wind blew on this occasion, Parl Dro caught a faroff curdle of yells and what sounded like stones landing hard on wood.

He was not particularly in favor of this, nor did it worry him unduly. Just as Ciddey's beauty, insidious and not instantly apparent, had interested, but not spontaneously moved him.

On the return journey of the witch-hunting party to the village, Dro identified for the first time the thief-musician's varied regalia in their midst. As soon as they reached the juncture where the village thoroughfare branched off from the road, the musician swung aside. Some of the villagers appeared to be arguing with him, but it looked good-natured enough. After a moment or so, the minstrel moved on into the fields that lined the opposite side of the road. Dro lost sight of the man cutting south through a strand of young wheat.

Afternoon streamed over the landscape, tinting everything with its unmistakable changes of light.

Relaxed, yet unsleeping, Dro sat with his back to a tree, watching the village with a long-lidded gaze. His mantle was laid aside, revealing that trousers, boots, shirt were also black, black as his eyes, though his hair had mellowed a shade under the sun. He looked exotic, foreign and dangerous. Only a fool would have stolen up on him from behind. It appeared the man prowling up the south side of the slope was not quite such a fool as that.

The drab green lost itself in the grass, the poppy red did not. If he had been attempting surprise, the musician had obviously accepted his inadequacy at the game. He emerged quite flamboyantly to Dro's left, and stood studying him with frank accusation.

"I suppose you were expecting me," he said.

Dro looked at him. The look was neither baleful nor encouraging.

"You could *pretend* to be astounded," said the musician. "It wouldn't kill you."

"It might have killed you," said Dro.

The musician shrugged and trudged the rest of the way up the slope. When he stood directly over Dro, he produced the bag of pebbles he had thieved the previous night. He threw it dramatically at Dro's feet.

"That was a nasty trick," said the musician.

"Stealing isn't particularly wholesome, either."

"You could survive it. You're famous. I'd never thieve from someone who couldn't afford to lose a few coins. How was I supposed to pay for my supper? You think I had credit there? They wanted me to play songs and pay money too."

Parl Dro sat looking down the slope.

The musician slung the musical instrument off his back on its frayed embroidered sling, and set it in the grass. He sat down about a foot from Dro.

"In the end," he said, "I had to make up to some girl to get a bed for the night. And I was worn out, so *that* wasn't a good idea. But I'd better stop. I can see I'll have you in tears in a minute."

Dro went on gazing at the village.

The musician lay back in the grass and gazed at the leaves overhead, spotted sheer green against sheer blue. His face, with its long nose and cap of darkly gilded hair, was basically a rather sad and very worried face, from some angles quite ordinary, from others extremely good-looking, from others still, simply mournful.

"You probably want to know why I'm here," he said at length.

"Not especially."

"All right. You want to know why I'm not clever enough to clear off." The silence lasted. "All right," said the minstrel, "I'll tell you. We're actually going the same way."

"Which way is that?"

"Oh, come on. The way any of your calling was bound to go, this year or next. Of course, it may only be a legend. In which case, it's still my business. I can still make a song of it. I'm referring to Ghyste Mortua."

"Someone you know," said Parl Dro.

"A *place* we *both* know. If it exists. I've been roaming up and down these parts quite a few days, trying to suss it out. Or find someone who knows the way. I'd take a gamble you do."

"Would you?"

"You see, in my sort of career, you need a song to make your name. One unique, marvelous, never-to-be-successfully-plagiarized song. It came to me, one night when I was really down—I mean *really* down—on my luck, that my song was in Ghyste Mortua. Not that I'm one of these courageous idiots who'll run his neck into a noose for a two-penny piece. Myal Lemyal, which is me, is the cautious type. And I know when I need guidance. As for you, you might like some music on the road."

"And then again," said Dro softly, "I might not."

"And then again you might not. Incidentally, about that girl in the old house, I consider the trouble you've caused her stinks. I went down there with some of them. They were bellowing that you'd gone, but they hadn't, and they were throwing stones at her door. You're not a particularly splendid hero, are you?"

Dro smiled.

"Compared with you?"

"Oh well, if you're going to be offensive."

Idly, Myal Lemyal sat up and picked the instrument off the grass. It was an eccentric package, the main portion being a body and sound box of grotesquely painted wood with chips of ivory set in, from which mass two necks extended, each strung with fine wires that crisscrossed each other midway. Across the top of these necks ran a bar to which tarnished silver pegs skewered certain of the sets of wire strings at apparently random points. Meanwhile, straight through the bar and into the sound box ran a wooden reed with a mouthpiece of ivory. The stops followed the reed down through the bole of the instrument in such a way that, as Myal Lemyal shortly demonstrated, agile fingers could manage both strings and stops simultaneously. The performance, analyzed, should have been quite impossible, additionally so when, with a precarious balance achieved against his shoulder, and eight fingers and two thumbs scuttling over each other in all directions, he set his lips to the ivory mouthpiece. His hair skidded at once into his eyes, which seemed to have crossed. He looked both maniacal and preposterous. While from the unholy instrument came the sounds of paradise. Of harps that were panpipes, of lutes that were also flutes, of mandolins that were also lyres and trumpets, of celestial, never-before-dreamed-of melody, harmony, counterpoint and rhythm.

When he finished, slipping off the string again, he laid the instrument in the grass once more, and peered at it melancholically. The slope seemed to go on singing to itself for quite some while.

"As you said," Myal ventured, "you might not care for music."

"I was only curious," said Parl Dro, "as to why such genius needs to be out picking pockets in the wilderness."

"Genius?" Myal smiled. The smile was angelic. He looked noble, even very beautiful, but the illusion vanished quickly. "Well, you know how it is."

"Did you steal the instrument, too?"

"I? Oh no. My father did that. He killed a man to get it, and the man, I assume, put a bane on him, and on me, I shouldn't wonder. My father used to beat sparks out of me every time he got drunk, which was pretty frequent. When he was sober, he'd teach me to play that. I hate my father. I'm not that keen on myself."

He lapsed into a moody reverie, staring where the dark man, who looked like handsome Death, was still watching the village, the road, the mountain. Soon, Myal lay down in the grass again.

"What'll you do about that girl, that Ciddey Soban?"

"What do you think?"

"Go back and make her miserable some more. Push her dead sister out of this world into the next, so they can both be nicely lonely and wretched."

Something pecked at his hand. Fearing snakes, Myal jerked three feet backward, landed, and saw the flask Dro had been offering him. He accepted the flask gingerly, uncorked it and sniffed. An appreciative grin, unlike the smile, altered the desolation of his face.

"White brandy. Haven't tasted that since I was on the Cold Earl's lands."

He tasted it, and kept on tasting it. Dro let him.

They said a few more things to each other, on Myal's side progressively unintelligible. Bees came and went in patches of clover. Large grape-dark clouds with edges of gold tissue clotted together behind the mountain.

"Why'd you do it?" Myal Lemyal asked. "Why'd you send um out of thissorld wheney doan wanna go?"

"Why does a surgeon draw a man's tooth when it's decayed?"

"Issen the same. Not attall. I've heard of you, and your *kind*. Poor liddle ghosts driven sobbinganscreaming out'f the place they wanna be most."

"It's necessary. What's dead can't go on pretending it's alive."

"Anthasswhy you wannagetter Ghyzemortwa—"

When the light began to go, Myal Lemyal was already gone, blind drunk on white brandy and passed out in the clover. Senseless, however, one hand had fallen on the sling of the grotesque instrument, and mingled with it in a firm and complex clutch.

Of Parl Dro there was no longer any sign.

When he woke and saw the stars scattered like dice overhead, Myal knew he had made yet another mistake.

There was a clean fragrant wind blowing on the hills. It helped soothe his pounding headache. But it did not help much in the other matter. He had lost the King of Swords, handsome Death, Parl Dro the Ghost-Killer. Of course, it was inevitable that he would ruin this chance too. Myal considered his first slip-up had been in getting born. He had gone on wrecking his chances systematically ever since.

The worst thing was that he was still drunk. Despite the headache and an inevitable queasiness, he still felt inclined to roll about in the grass howling with insane laughter. His own inanity irritated him. He put the instrument on his shoulder and staggered down the slope, alternately giggling and cursing himself.

He was detouring by the village and stumbling across the fields to rejoin the road beyond it, making for the faintly glowing cutout of the mountain, before it dawned on him why. Though Dro had abandoned him, Dro would not have abandoned the leaning house and its two sisters, one quick, one dead. Sooner or later Dro would be revisiting that house. Myal had only to be in the vicinity to freshen their acquaintance. Perhaps another tack might be in order. "I never had a big brother. Never had anyone to look up to, learn from." He could hear himself saying it, and winced. It was difficult to be sure how to bet around someone like Dro.

The house was leaning there, in its accustomed position of decline, when he reemerged on the road. Starlit, the moon still asleep, and dominated by its trees, it did look ghostly.

Myal shivered, scared and also romantically stirred by the idea. He had glimpsed the live sister, Ciddey, five evenings ago, when he first exhaustedly arrived here over the mountain. She was a true lady, like one of the Cold Earl's women, or the Gray Duke's, or a damsel of any of those endless succession of courts he had flitted in and out of, mothlike, scorching his wings. Ciddey was like a moth too. Pale, exquisite, fragile. And somehow inimical, eerie . . . abroad by night with unhuman glittering eyes—

Myal began to know the itching panic of a babe alone in unfamiliar darkness.

He looked at the house among its trees, and hugged himself in an infantile intuitive search for comfort. Naturally, Parl Dro would come along the road and find him this way, quivering with fright. But there was as yet no evidence of Dro or his inexorable exorcism.

Suddenly Myal had a wild impulse. He was accustomed to them; they were usually misguided and mostly led to mishap. Their phenomena had also commenced with him in childhood. The perverse directives the brain was sometimes capable of—to drop the tray loaded with priceless glass, to leap the too-wide gap between a pair of speeding wagons, to spit in the face of the landowner's steward—such contrary notions, normally suppressed by the average person, had always proved irresistible to Myal. They were not caused by reckless bravery, either, for Myal was not brave, but merely by the same chemistry that had forced him, so unwisely, to be conceived.

The current impulse was driving him across the road, toward the iron gate, into the umber yard. That achieved, he sat, trembling slightly, on the edge of the stone well. He swung the instrument forward, and began to sing Ciddey (or was it Cilny?) a love song. His voice was an unpowerful but attractive tenor. In the silence it seemed very loud. The strings popped under his fingers, and the notes struck the walls like uncanny sideways rain.

When the shutter slapped open overhead, Myal's heart practically stopped.

He glanced up, keeping the song going. A pallid bolt of light hung in the ivy, the shape of a single moth's wing.

The girl leaned through the light. It was the live one— probably. Her braided hair was like moonshine.

Myal gasped and left off singing. He was half in love with her, and frozen with fear.

"What is it?" said the girl. She stared at the instrument. Slender little hands like fox paws gripped the sill. "What do you want?"

"I want," Myal swallowed and lost his head completely. "I want to warn you."

"Don't trouble. I know the village. They'll behave themselves. They still respect the name of Soban."

"I don't mean that. I mean the man called Dro." He heard her catch her breath. She was lovely. He wished he was a thousand miles away. "He made out he was leaving, but he'll be back—if he isn't back already. He was going to Ghyste Mortua—I think. But he reckons he's got dealings to settle with you first. You and—your sister."

"Go away!" cried the girl in the window.

Myal jumped, but felt more familiar ground under his feet at her tone of anger and threat.

"Only trying to be helpful. Sorry I spoke."

"Wait," said the girl. She was suddenly, appallingly defenseless. "What do you know about him?"

"Only that he'll be back. If you want my advice, not that you do, you'd run for it."

"Where could I go?"

"Maybe—with me."

He stared up at her, shivering at the romance of it all and wishing he could shut himself up. To his chagrin and his relief, the girl laughed at him.

"*You.* Who are *you*? Besides, what about my dead sister? Where is *she* to go? With you, too?"

"Perhaps," Myal shuddered, "Parl Dro made an error there. Perhaps I don't believe in ghosts."

A shriek slit down the night.

It came from the topmost room of the tower, on the north side of the house.

Myal and Ciddey were momentarily petrified. The girl broke from her rigor before he did. Leaving the shutter wide, she turned and ran away into the depth of the house.

Myal remained in the yard, glaring wildly between the trees at the one corner of the tower that was visible from this vantage, a constriction in his throat.

CHAPTER THREE

———••———◆———•———

The trees around the house on its north side could have been deliberately planted to give access to the tower. One in particular rested its boughs almost across the sill of the second-story window. Of course, a lame man might not be reckoned capable of scaling trees.

When Parl Dro reached the window, he found it latched from within. Easing the lame leg, which itself did not reckon it should be required to scale trees, Dro produced a slender knife, and slid it through the join between the shutters. In a couple of seconds it had raised the latch, and the two panes of dull glass parted. The room beyond was bare and empty, save for a few skeletal plants dying in dry soil and cracked pots on the floor. Dro entered it and vacated it as swiftly. The possible significance of the pots—herbal witchery—did not concern him, nor any longer the witch, judging by the state of them. Dro moved out through the door onto a steep stair. The top room lay straight above him at the stairhead, closed by a thick wooden door with plates and lock of rusty iron.

The girl was in the house, for he had seen her there soon after sunset, going with her lamp from window to window, latching each. The light had ultimately come to rest in an upper room, a thin thread behind shutters of wood. It was possible that this was a ruse, but he did not judge her so devious as to leave her lamp barely obvious in one place, and creep to another through the pitch-dark house. Besides, she would be hoping he was gone.

Just as he was starting up the tower stair, he heard the poignant unmistakable notes of Myal Lemyal's wire strings.

Interested, Dro checked, almost pleased. If anything, this was to the good; Myal playing troubador at one end of the building would distract Ciddey Soban from this one. On the other hand, Myal's purpose was decidedly oblique, maybe even to himself. It had been straightforward to dupe the musician, yet almost simultaneously, he had shown himself possessed of both talent and cunning—a talent and cunning he appeared bored with: or even unaware of. Not every man could have tracked Parl Dro to his cover on the slope that day, and not every man had ambitions connected to Ghyste Mortua. Nor did every minstrel make such music.

The current theme was trivial but not displeasing. Dro listened to it with a quarter ear as he finished the climb up the rest of the stairs, and picked the iron lock of the door at the top with his knife.

When he got into the room, he forgot the music.

The aura of the manifested dead was intense and total. That pervasion, like an odor of cold stale perfume. That feel of an invisible active center, which strove to draw off the energies of life, and of the living, into itself. No wonder Ciddey Soban was pale and slight. His earliest training had taught him that, even where love caused the deadalive to linger, they sucked the vitality of the quick who harbored them. They could not help it, any more than fire could help destroying a stick of wood put into the hearth. It merely happened. It merely had to be stopped.

Sometimes Parl Dro had been paid large sums of money to perform such work as this. Other times, he had slunk in like a thief, as he did now, and sharp pebbles had struck him across the back when the task was done.

The physical aspect of the room was itself depressingly invocational.

It was a bedchamber, or had been arranged to be: A stark canopied bed, maiden narrow, with fluted white drapes. A

carved chest, in which he had no doubt Cilny Soban's garments lay carefully folded amid bags of herbs. An antique
mirror of polished silver stood on the chest, and two or three
old books. On the inside of the door he had closed hung
some tiny charms on a thread. Some of them looked like a
baby's teeth. In a bony chair sat a child's doll, made of wood
with cannily jointed limbs. It was dressed in faded spectral
white, like everything else, and had long lank hair of flaxen
wool. There was a tapestry on the wall, a rug on the floor, a
table with an ewer and basin, some little combs chased with
imitation mother-of-pearl, and an open ivory casket with delicate beads and bangles in it.

It was a sad room, and very horrible. It provided the perfect compost from which a ghost might ferment itself and es-
tablish its false claims on an earthly existence.

In the darkest corner, something stood off the rug, on the
floor. It was a slim, two-foot-high stone jar.

The moment he looked at the jar, he felt her seep into the
room. She had not been there when he entered. Cilny had
died in the spring, not so long ago. She might need a human
presence to rouse her. But also he suspected Ciddey had
warned her into hiding. Even now, she was reluctant to
evolve, sensing antipathy. A desire for his company, love,
even fear, she could feed on. Dro offered none of these. Yet
now, looking at the pot which held her ashes, he began to ex-
ert his will on her. He began to drag her, willing or not, into
the room.

His spine and the roots of his hair registered her arrival before his eyes did. But in less than half a minute, he could see
her quite plainly too.

Frail and blonde she was, mostly transparent. No, she was
not a very strong deadalive. She wore the clothing of her
death hour, which was quite usual, the long flimsy nightgown
the villagers had described, though for some reason the wreath
of flowers was absent. Then, in the way of ghosts, unexpectedly
and piteously, she touched him—by folding her arms shyly
about herself. It was the modesty of a very young girl who
had never slept with a man, and discovered herself alone with
one in her nightwear. Nor was it contrived; he was fairly sure
of that. He said to her gently, "Don't be afraid, Cilny. Do
you know who I am?"

Her voice was hardly more than a rustle, dry papers or blown leaves.

"Ciddey told me of a man, a lame man in black."

"What did she say?"

"That you'd kill me."

"Cilny," he said quietly, "how can I kill you? You're already dead."

"No," she cried in her rustling voice. Panic made it stronger. "No—no—" She stared at him. "Ciddey woke me. I was asleep, and she woke me."

"She shouldn't have awakened you. You would have awakened in your own time, and gone on your own way, to the place you have to go to."

"No. I'll stay here. I want my sister. I want Ciddey."

He did not wish to be rough with her. Sometimes it was possible to comfort, to smooth the path. The going through could be calm, even in some cases blissful, thankful. But this one would plead and whimper at him. He was steeled to the hurt, but to prolong the hurt for her would be no sort of kindness.

He took a step toward the pot of ashes, and then the ghost-girl shrieked.

The shriek had attained a dumbfounding strength. It thrilled through the room, through his ears, through stone. He knew Ciddey would have heard it.

Dro lunged toward the jar. To reach it, he had to go right by the ghost, partly through her. A debilitating chill sank over him as he did so. But he paid no attention to it. He kneeled and wrenched off the cover of the jar and threw it away. She came all about him in that moment, a white gale, a pale insect whipping him with frantic opalescent wings. Primeval horror strangled him, swarmed over his skin. He could smell only the grave, and phosphorescent worms crawled across his eyes. He wanted—needed—to lash out, beat her insubstantiality away, run yelling from the room—well-known sensations he was accustomed to controlling.

Vaguely, beyond it all, he heard a door flung open lower in the tower.

Her ashes were Cilny's link to mortal life.

The link had always to be destroyed, or at least altered. The means were as various as the links themselves. The bone must be smashed, air mingled with its fragments. The scarf,

the glove must be charred in fire, flames mingled with the
cloth. Change was the key.

The ashes lay far down in the stone pot. He could see
them, even through the whirlwind of pallor and dark. He
unhooked the flask of white brandy from his belt and pulled
the cork. Luckily, it did not take very much to render Myal
Lemyal drunk. There was enough left for this enterprise.

Dro poured the libation with a careful steady hand, covering all the floor of the jar. There was a brief smoke, as if
from acid.

Suddenly the swirling nightmare dispersed from about him.
It was as if a great noise had fallen silent.

He stood up slowly, and looking around he saw Cilny's
face staring at him, huge-eyed, desperate, but it was the doll
in the chair. Cilny was gone.

She had not cried out again. Perhaps she could not summon the power. Or perhaps, at the very last, she had seen beyond the gate, seen that the land she must journey to was
unknown, alien, yet not terrible after all, not to be feared.

For a second, Parl Dro felt weak and drained to the
threshold of illness. At such times, his will expended like a
loss of blood, he was inclined to believe the adage that for
every ghost a ghost-killer returned to its death, he moved
himself a day nearer to his own.

He leaned his shoulder on the wall and watched the door,
waiting for it to burst wide. Which it presently did.

The two sisters were very similar, yet Cilny had had an
elusive quality Ciddey did not. Or was it only that Ciddey's
elusiveness was more quickly translatable?

She darted a white raging glare about the chamber. She did
not ask why he was there, or what he had done. She knew,
naturally. She too would scent the vacancy where the dank
perfume of the ghost had lain so heavy.

"I'm sorry," he said. He was not. It was a courtesy, and
really just a facet of his perverseness to offer it. For this was
no hour for courtesies.

The girl reacted in a shocking, predictable fashion. She
launched herself straight at him, actually springing off her
feet toward his face or throat like an attacking cat. It should
have been nothing to catch and hold her, but she had acquired the force and fury of the possessed. Two nails raked
down his cheek before he got her hands. Probably fortunately

she was too naive, well-bred or fastidious to aim the traditional kick at him any street woman could have taught her.

When he did have hold of her, she struggled, struggles which ran down like clockwork as her violence ran out. Then she wept, and he held her through that, too. It did not always happen this way, but sometimes it did. He no longer bothered to assess what he felt at such an instant. Years before he would have identified regret, guilt, compassion; even self-satisfaction, even sex. But all these twinges of aftermath were basically meaningless. He let them travel their course, like the girl's tears, mainly unheeding, completely uninfluenced. It was a kind of ritual.

When she eventually pushed away from him as fiercely as if she meant to strike at him again, that was ritual too.

She walked across the room to the chair. She lifted the doll and sat down with it, taking it on her lap. She looked at the doll.

"Well," she said, "you got what you came for." Her voice was choked from crying, but otherwise completely level. "I do trust you don't expect paying for it."

"No."

Abruptly she tossed the doll off her lap onto the floor. She looked at the floor then.

"Such a great man," she said. "So erudite. So clever."

Parl Dro limped toward the door. Ciddey said, "I want you to meet someone who—"

"Don't dirty your mouth with a lot of gutter phrases you don't properly understand," he said. "It won't make any difference. To either of us."

She waited until he was through the door, then she called softly, "Have you ever thought about how many must loathe you, how many must wish you ill, want your suffering and your despair? Don't you ever feel it on your back, don't you ever feel it in your belly, eating you alive, Parl Dro?"

He began to go down the stairs. He wondered if she would call out to him again. It seemed likely she would.

In fact, she waited till he was in the yard, going under the dead fig tree. He had hesitated briefly. Starlight filmed the well as on the previous night and, as on the previous night, there still lingered there that intangible aura of unnaturalness. Her voice drifted from the tower, gathering the aura about itself. The sentences fell like ugly fruits onto the ground. Her gutter vocabulary was better than he would have anticipated. When she finished, he had reached the gate, but though her voice was low, he had not missed a word.

Myal Lemyal had presumably taken to his heels at some juncture, or else concealed himself with exceptional cunning, for there was no hint of him within the yard or outside.

Dro stepped back onto the road, and turned eastward.

The village, when he went by it again half a mile farther on, seemed unfamiliar and smaller than before; he saw it with a stranger's eye. Since tonight he did not intend to stay there, it had acquired the closed and unwelcoming facade of a plane that offered no shelter.

Myal Lemyal had certainly removed himself from the scene. In his own haphazard way, he was as sensitive to the atmospheres of deadaliveness as any ghost-killer, though failing to interpret them in positive terms, and with, very decidedly, no compulsion to engage them in battle.

His neurasthenic fascination with the whole venture had, however, increased. It was often the case with him that what frightened him most he would run headlong after—a habit he deplored but had been unable to break himself of.

Dro also fascinated and frightened him to a colossal extent. Myal, additionally, had convinced himself that Dro was an essential ingredient in the brilliant plan to find Ghyste Mortua, that—possibly—apocryphal domain of the undead.

So when the house's sense of manifestation and emotional frenzy were epitomized in the supernatural shriek, Myal quickly pulled himself together and ran. But not very far. He had simply leaped up the nearest slope like a scared rabbit and dropped in the thick grass there, panting and appalled. Ten minutes later, when he had dared himself to raise his head, he realized with some self-blind surprise that he could still see the lopsided roof of the house below.

It seemed inspired, then, to set himself to watch the spot for further developments. The watch was not a long one. Parl Dro's brandy and Myal's nervous exhaustion, combined with the sprint up the slope, proved conclusive. About one minute before Dro walked out of the gate and back onto the road, Myal was sprawled, head on arms, soundly asleep.

A little after midnight, when the adolescent moon hung itself over his head like a piece of broken plate, Myal stirred, accepted the new mistake, cursed it, and fell asleep again. He too was not unused to slumbering on bare ground. But he dreamed first of his mother whom he had never known, and then of his drunken father and the leather strap known too well, and twitched and muttered and sighed.

Just before dawn, he rolled part of the way down the slope and came up against a young fir tree. Through the branches and the warp and woof of the grass, he saw a bank of pigeon-blue cloud barricading the eastern horizon, the light coming pale and mysterious above it.

There was no sound anywhere but the drift of the wind over the land, and the watery drips and trickles of birdsong. Then a door slammed like a wooden drum, below at the leaning house.

Myal stared down past the stem of the fir tree.

Ciddey Soban, white as porcelain, came out of the shadows and the trees and turned toward him. For a minute, he thought she meant to come straight up the incline, but then she went away from the house, the road and Myal's slope, passing under the shoulders of the uplands, going north.

Myal's heart thumped. He got up and combed his hair with his long fingers, and straightened the instrument on its frayed sling across his shoulders. With an awareness of vague dread, he walked around the curve of the hill, squinting forward until he had her pallid figure in sight again. Maintaining the distance between them, he followed her. He had a vile notion why he must, and his eyes were wet already.

She had sat in Cilny's chair all night, and thought of Parl Dro the Ghost-Killer, and how she hated him.

Sometimes thoughts of Cilny, or occasionally of her own self, would interrupt these reveries. Sometimes she thought even of their father, his absurd botching together of things to sell as strange artifacts. That was perhaps inevitable. But she did not consider any of these matters for more than a second or so.

She began by wishing Parl Dro dead, and in her mind she constructed the way of it, now one way, now another. She pictured him stabbed and smothered, she pictured him buried alive in earth, or hanged, or torn in shreds by animals, wolves or bears or cats. In various of these fantasies she was physically present, instigating and directing them. Later he met deaths with slower and more subtle formulae, and then she was not there. Later still, she did not think of his death at all, only of him. He had been far younger than she had expected, from the stories. She imagined to herself his youth, his childhood, his birth even. She imagined his old age still to come; sickness and poverty, wealth and loneliness and joy—all his, and she was almost impartial now. She came, in the last descent of night, to behold him as a life, separate from her, a man, an entity. Her hate was no longer a force directed against him. Her hate had become Parl Dro. He stood like a black tree against a backdrop of pure nothingness. She could think of no other thing.

When the birds began to tell off their notes to the lightening sky, Ciddey rose. For a moment, she was unsure of where she meant to go, and why. Then she recalled, with a dry ebbing at her heart, how everything was settled, that she had no need to concern herself with plans. She had only to act.

Outside, a bar of cloud lay low on the horizon, like another hill behind the hills. The mountain glistened, cool and sculptured, in the preludes of the morning.

As she walked along the rims of the slopes, treading north, the dark started to lift, in level sweeps, like flocks of birds flying up from the land. These things were so known to her. The lift and fall of day and night, the mountain, the country. She seemed only a figment of everything that was, only a memory of some other girl who had lived long in this place.

From a rise, quite soon, she saw the stream shining before her.

The yellow asphodel of the spring was gone from its banks. She glanced about bewilderedly, searching for some token flower, but there were only summer daisies in the grass. Nor was the stream as clear as in the spring. It was tinged with the brown clay that lined the channel. Nor did it flow so swiftly as when the melted snow, from the high shelves of its source, ran with it.

Ciddey took off her shoes, as if she meant to go wading in the stream. She set them neatly, side by side, on the bank.

The night chill, retained by the water, made her gasp as she stepped into it. For an instant, she felt incapable of continuing the deed. She stood shivering, balanced against the syrupy freezing push of the current, looking wildly about her. Almost at once, a man appeared on the rise beyond the bank, about eighty feet away. It was the man who had sung under her window the night before, who must have done so at the order of Parl Dro to distract her. Fate had directed him.

She stared at the man and he at her. Suddenly he began to wave his arms, one green, one red, and to shout. Then he began to rush toward her down the slope, and the instrument jounced behind him.

He must not reach her in time.

Ciddey let herself fall directly back into the stream. The cold liquid came over her face, entering her nostrils and eyes. She did not strike the stream bed hard, the water was too buoyant. Already it raised her and bore her forward. She was not yet leaden enough to sink and to lie still.

Her braids were coming undone. She should have rebound them. She had not thought to.

She had held her breath, but now she breathed, and let the stunning cold darkness into herself. She was so cold now that she no longer felt it at all.

Somewhere far away she heard the man scrabbling in the stream, not at the right spot, for the current had moved her quite some distance.

Everything slid away, almost gently now. All but one thing. She understood she must not let go of that.

The very last sight she had, before all human seeing went out of her, was of the two black eyes of Parl Dro. They seemed to draw her from herself, right out of her bursting, suffocating flesh. Her consciousness, narrowed to a thread, passed through them as through the eyes of needles. Her hatred was so fine, she felt a pang of exultation. Then she was a feather floating on a tide in darkness. And then she died.

Upstream, Myal Lemyal, plunging knee-high in the icy water, drenched himself and thrashed the shallow race with his hands. By the time he found her, he was already half mad.

He dragged her out onto the bank. Her face was swollen and pop-eyed, as if she had been strangled. He retched with terror, but threw her on this bloated face and tried to squeeze the water out of her.

Finally he gave over. He left her lying face down in a veil of pale hair. The soles of her small bare feet, very clean and faintly pink, flushed pinker as the sunrise burned down on them.

Myal sat on the bank some yards away from her, gnawing his nails. He did not look at her beyond intermittent, furtive glances. Eventually, he swung the musical instrument around on its sling into the crook of his shoulder.

He made a song for Ciddey Soban. He did not know how beautiful it was. But the instrument had been wetted by his career through the stream, and some of the strings sagged and gradually became flat. If his father had been with him, Myal would have been beaten.

In the end, Myal stopped playing. He put his arms around the instrument, hugging it tightly, and watched the stream going by.

An hour or so later, the cold in his still dripping boots and shirt started to wriggle its way under his ribs and spine. He sneezed and rubbed his hand across his eyes and stood up. And found he was standing on one of Ciddey's small shoes.

He walked away from the stream slowly.

He could hear cows mooing like bassoons across the curves of the land. The odor of turf and flowers became an irresistible series of irritations in the passages behind his nose and throat, and he sneezed again and cursed himself and the world, and trudged once more toward the eastern snarl of the road.

CHAPTER FOUR

———•×———×•———

Five miles east of the village, the landscape began to flow steadily downward. Deep valleys appeared and shimmering ravines. Trees like poles, each with a solitary rounded cloud of foliage smoldering at its top, led in avenues along the crests of ridges, or by the misty lanes of faraway, indeterminate rivers.

Somewhere in this country, by night, Parl Dro had slept, wrapped in his black mantle. The weather had been soft and warm, turning cold only as the dawn approached. But a few hours after sunrise, the heat came back, smilingly, as if its absence might be overlooked.

On the morning wall of a farm, a skinny child sat, dangling its legs among the vines. When it suddenly saw the black-clad man striding his long lame strides down the road, the child slunk into a thicket. It sprang out at him as he passed.

"Give me some money!"

Dro did not look at it. "Why?"

"I have the magic sight," said the child. "I'll tell your future. Give me a twenty-penny piece."

Dro stopped. He looked at the child. It was a girl with sun-bleached hair. He threw her a twenty-penny piece, spinning it lazily from his height to hers. She caught the coin, and said, "I know who you are. I thought you were a legend. They said you'd be by this way sometime."

"Who said?"

"They all did. For years and years. Now I'll tell you. Watch out. Before and behind. You've got a lot of enemies."

"Have I really?" said Dro.

"But not me," said the child. "I think you're lovely."

She ran away along the wall. Rosy dust puffed from the ground as she went. The soil was more acrid here, and powdery.

At noon there was an inn that sold wine and golden cheese. Peaches ripened on the walls. A blind dog sunned itself, and whined when Parl Dro's shadow slid over its back.

In the afternoon, the road shifted to the south. A thread of track beat on eastwards, but faded in a molasses-colored wood as the sun began to wester. When he emerged from the wood, the land sloped down to a loop of one of the misty rivers. A ruined fortress stood dreamily in the loop, melting into the sky as sunset condensed the air. A village lay along the river's edge. It had the usual wide street, supplemented by a couple of others almost as wide. The sewage-dispelling water courses appeared to discharge into an area of marsh that strained out of the river to the north. A dab of smoke coiled from the roofs. Some fishing boats lay, themselves like spread fish, side by side on the shore.

The premonition he had been having, inchoate but persistent, was now so strong Dro avoided the village completely. He walked instead diagonally, clipping the marsh. A causeway of pleached bricks went through mud and strips of water, out onto the baked meadow in the loop of the river where the fortress was.

The outer walls had crumbled. The inner had a lovely smoothness, sanded down by the elements. Some earl or princeling had lorded it here one or two hundred years ago, master of the river. Nobody much came here now. No paths were worn across the meadow. Not even goats or sheep had been pastured, for the grass was virgin and proud. Probably the village reckoned the fortress to be haunted. It had that look to it, secretive, smoky. Only a ghost-killer like Dro could have told for sure that there were no ghosts. It was just an empty shell.

A wind blew up along the river, and the chill came back with the dusk. Dro set a fire inside the lee of the inner wall, where a staircase went up into a vault of sky. A wild apple tree had rooted in the earth by the stair, with precocious green fruit on it. He put a couple to bake out their sourness in the ashes around the fire.

A huge owl, soundless, like a paper kite, sailed over the meadow to its hunting.

Parl Dro sat against the wall. He had only to wait awhile. He was alert, but very still. It was a knack of his, one of many disciplines, to be able to turn off awareness of time, and all superfluous senses, resting them, as he rested the crippled leg. Every day of walking on the roads was a day of fighting that pain, and every respite brought a dizzying relief. Done in, he paid little attention to either condition or cause.

Then, through half-closed eyes, he saw a woman mantled in gold hair, leaning to his firelight. She was very real, but when he raised his lids, no longer there.

The child at the farm had triggered certain memories, one familiar and crucial. He thought about it, turning the past over in his mind, as he waited for the present to catch up to him.

His father had been a soldier in some small border war big enough to kill him. Parl Dro's mother had died awhile later, when he was about four years of age. The local landowner kept a house where homeless children might grow up in reasonable conditions. When he was ten, Dro was already working in the fields. But, because he had shown some aptitude for learning, the landowner, much fairer than most, sent him twice a week into town, to be schooled.

The school was ramshackle. In winter, icicles formed high on the indoor beams under the attic where the roof leaked. The children would huddle around an iron pot with coals in it. There were fifty boys and about fifteen girls whose relatives thought them odd enough to need lessons. All but one of the girls were alien creatures, whose nurses always came with them. In winter, they brought their own iron firepots, too. The last girl was poor and came alone. She sat bolt upright in a clean ragged darned dress. Her hair was always clean, too, a long fair flag that hung down her back and onto

the bench. The well-off little girls would not speak to her.
They had remarked loudly to each other that she was a
hussy, having no nurse to guard her. The poor girl remarked
as loudly, to the air, that she, being virtuous and trustworthy,
required no guard, as they plainly did.

Dro saw her twice a week, each of the two days that he
came to the school, for three years. Then, one day when he
was thirteen, he suddenly noticed her. She would play dice
games with the boys, which she usually won, and run races
with them, which sometimes she won. She would also climb
trees, though not in company with the boys, for she expressed
the opinion that this would be unseemly. The day Parl Dro
noticed her was an evening in early summer. He came out
into the field behind the school and saw her sitting in an
apple tree. The sun spilled down her hair like molten honey.
She was talking to herself, or to the birds, or the tree. He
climbed an adjacent tree and sat and looked at her. She did
not seem offended or abashed when she saw him. They began
to converse quite easily. What they spoke about was unrecall-
ed and meaningless. It might have been books or the state of
the crops.

When he came back to the town on his next school day, he
arrived early, and walked slowly by her house. It was a tiny
hovel, held up mainly by two other hovels at either side of it.
Yet it was the cleanest hovel for miles around. When she
came out she did not seem amazed to see him. Her only kin
was a grandmother, who that morning had been baking. The
girl had two slices of warm crackling bread, spread with dripping, one of which she presented graciously to Parl with the
compliments of the house.

She had a name, but he never called her by it. Her
nickname, which her grandmother had given her for her hair,
was "Silky." Parl and the grandmother, but no one else,
called her that.

Through the summer, they spent a lot of time together.
Sometimes they played truant from the school. They roved
about the hills. They talked of myths, legends bound up with
the land, and ancient times when emperors had ruled em-
pires there, and women with hot blood had ridden over it to
battle. He showed her how to catch fish in the streams. She
told him he was cruel to catch fish he did not need to eat.
Later, when the grandmother suffered a setback in her

meager life style, Silky begged him to show her again how to catch fish. They took the catch back to the hovel together, the color of river pebbles and fine to eat, particularly when starvation was the alternative. He stole bread for them, Silky and the grandmother, from the landowner's ovens. When times grew fatter, Silky, by way of repayment, stole a knife for him from the steelsmith's. Parl had a little trouble replacing it in the forge before it was missed. They were very young, and their sexuality was limited by their youth, their situation and their codes of honor regarding each other. But they learned certain lessons of fire together, light fierce kisses, the rapidity of a heartbeat, hands and bodies and the press of summer grass. There would have been more, if things had evolved differently.

When the harvest came due, the landowner called in all his workers to the fields. For three or four weeks, Parl would not see the school, the town, or Silky. They parted gravely, as if for a year, beneath the apple tree in the field behind the school.

The harvest went as it always did, which was back-breakingly, but well. The weather was hot and the sheaves like tinder, and men were posted to keep watch for fires. At night, Parl fell asleep in the open, the stars dazzling overhead. The air smelled of grapes and wine and scythed grain. Fireflies sprinkled the bushes. He hardly thought of Silky, comforted that he did not need to think of her, because she would be there for him when he returned.

In the last week of the harvest there was a storm. Roaring and trampling, it tore down on the fields like a gigantic animal. Great smacks of wind clapped the corn flat to the ground. Lightning drove steel bolts through the earth. A tree blazed up on a hill, exploding with white electric fire and noise.

They worked against the gale and the lightning. When the rain came, they worked against that. Purple and wailing in the wind, the fields surrendered themselves to destruction. The last of the harvest was taken by the storm.

Somehow worse than the material loss, the threat of reduced rations, cut wages, which must inevitably follow, was a primitive distress which fell over all of them. The storm was like some supernatural show of wrath, sent as if to punish them, as if to demonstrate that however settled life might seem, nothing was certain. It was no surprise to Parl when the landowner, riding by him through the sodden ruin of the stacks, tapped his shoulder. "No more school for you, boy. I'm sorry. I'll need you here."

It was another month before Parl could find the space or energy to make the two hours' trek to the town. And then he had to set off two hours before sunrise, hoping he would not be missed when the other boys and men turned out soon after dawn. Probably he would get a beating. The idea of it seemed very distant. There had begun to be a feeling of depression, almost of fear inside him. In the swift importunate way of the young, he knew where salvation lay, and had come to care less and less for anything else.

He even ran some of the miles. The dawn was just a phantom smudge of light along the hills when he reached the town, the gate not even open. He did not wait for it, but climbed in at a place he knew of, illegal and urgent. Then, coming to the alley where the neat hovel sparkled between its far from immaculate supports, a sudden peculiar reluctance overcame him.

He loitered, undecided, on the street, until a woman came out of a door farther down, water bucket in hand. She glanced at him, and a half-startled look spread over her face. Something in the look unnerved him utterly, though why he did not know. He turned and ran.

He ran straight to the field that backed the dilapidated school. Again, he could not have said why, perhaps because it was a reference point, because he had come most often that way in the past.

In the field, he did not know what to do with himself. A dreadful uneasy restless exhaustion was coming over him. His hands buzzed and were full of nerves like needles. Insects seemed to crawl along his scalp, under the hair. Then, walking stupidly, he came on the apple tree and checked. It was still not quite true dawn, the sky silvery but nothing much lit up. For a moment the hideousness of the tree was more illusion than fact. As he was staring at it, he heard Silky's voice call lightly across the twilight behind him.

He turned and there she was in her clean darned rags, her gossamer hair blowing.

"Hallo, Parl," she said, "I thought you never would come back."

He stared at her, as he had stared at the tree. When she started to come toward him, a monumental terror boiled up in him, as if his blood and all his bones had changed to blazing ice.

"I waited for you, Parl. I've waited, every time I could, here by the tree."

He found he had backed a step away. When he did so, her face seemed to tremble. He still could not work out what was wrong. Then suddenly, as before, he broke into a run. He raced out of the field, away from her and from the tree, and as he ran, he shouted, long blank wordless shouts.

He did not stop again until a door stopped him. He had rushed right into it, and was crashing there with his fists. His yells had started all the dogs in the neighborhood barking. Then the door opened and he almost fell through it. He recognized Silky's grandmother as if from a long way off, and so he realized which door he had been hammering on.

"Oh," she said. "Oh, someone told you."

She started to cry. He became aware that he was crying, too. She led him to a chair and she shut the door.

She did not tell him directly, for of course she supposed he knew. It was only by her elaborations of grief that he found out. On the night of the storm which wrecked the harvest, Silky had been lingering by the apple tree in the field behind the school. When lightning had struck the tree, it had struck Silky also. Silky was dead. She had been dead for more than a month.

The grandmother brewed a herbal tea, which once the three of them had drunk. Nobody could drink it now. She patently wanted to keep Parl with her. He had been so often with Silky that now he seemed to conjure the girl for the old woman. Then the grandmother went to a chest and brought out something mysteriously. Drawing near to him, she showed him a cloth packet and opened it to reveal a clot of shining threads.

"All I've got left of her," she said.

She had trimmed Silky's silken hair the very morning before she died. The lightning had left nothing much, stripping flesh and sweetness, as it had stripped the tree. But these fringes of hair the grandmother had, by sheer luck, retained. Now, with a supreme effort of sacrifice, she offered the packet to Parl.

The instant he saw the hair, he felt very sick. Truths that he would learn and reason for himself in later years, came to him now merely instinctively. He felt but did not know what the shorn hair represented, and what its power must be. He had not guessed yet what that power signified.

Even so, instinct ordered him. Though he almost cringed with revulsion, he took the packet of hair.

He sat, with the packet lying by him, most of the day, in Silky's grandmother's house. All that time they said hardly anything to each other. She did not think to ask him if he should be anywhere else. She had forgotten real life. And Parl, though he understood the world went on, the landowner and his fields and his anger, they were only dimly perceived, dimly remembered, events outside the bubble which enclosed him and the blasted apple tree and the dead girl and her shorn hair.

When the day began to drain away, he rose and politely said good-bye to the old woman.

As he was going to the field, he met three of his former fellow students from the school. They clustered around him, eager to commiserate, or, as it seemed to him then, to enjoy his pain. Finally, one said, "So-and-so told me the priests went to bless the ground where she was killed. So-and-so said she might not lie quiet." One of the others cuffed him, growing aware of sheer bad taste at last. They went away.

Bats fizzled over the field and dissolved in the darkness. The sky was overcast, and rain fell. The struck tree glowed strangely in the wet with a hard vitreous sheen.

After an hour, Silky came walking softly through the rain toward him.

She was strong. She looked very near mortal this time. Before, she had been mostly transparent. He felt the weird drawing, the drag of energy going out of himself to her. He had wanted her to be there, and the sense that he fed her existence was almost pleasant. But then again, somewhere inside himself, he shied from this pleasure, was revolted by it. When she stood close to him and put her hand on his arm, he grew cold, colder than he had ever been in his life. He could not actually feel any pressure of her fingers.

There was no mark on her of the lightning. There rarely ever was, as he would come to know, evidence of the positive wounds or bodily spasms of death upon a living ghost. Its whole revenance was a masquerade of life; it tended to be amnesiac about the instant of annihilation, even in the degree of camouflage.

They sat together on a flat-topped stone. They talked. Presently he took her hand, and this time her hand felt real.

She had been young and innocent. Perhaps it was her naïveté that made her do what next she did, a frank and honest desire that they should be together as equals. Some would cheat and trick from jealousy and vengeance, out of hatred for those whose lives were genuine, some never slew directly or intentionally, warming themselves at lives as if at fires. Silky had been honorable. What remained of her could not have altered, so cruelly, into a fiend.

She was thirteen. A lovely, generous, desperate child. No, it was her naïveté, her longing not to lose him, that had made her seek his death.

She said that they should go into the school. There was a side door which each knew how to open. The rain was falling still, and she said they must take shelter. He asked her, almost with embarrassment, if the rain could inconvenience her now. She smiled radiantly at him.

"No. See, my hair's quite dry, and my dress. But you're wet through."

He let her take him to the door, and he opened it. Not because he cared about the rain, but because she had seemed to want them to go inside.

They wandered about the benches and the chests. The books were piled untidily and the slates more so. A mouse pranced over the tiles. It had been eating the large candle which the tutor used to tell the time. The atmosphere was very dark, yet somehow Parl could see everything well. Even when the girl hurried up the narrow stair to the attic, he was able to follow her with ease.

The floor of the attic, which rested on the beams of the hall below, was mainly rotten from the leaking roof where the rain even now entered, and where the sprays of winter ice would poke through to drip slowly on the pupils' heads fifty feet below. The joists had long since cracked. The walls bulged. The pupils were forbidden to enter the attic.

Silky ran daintily over the unsafe floor. Old parchment and cobwebs lay about. Where Silky's feet passed over them they left no imprint.

At his first step after her, a plank groaned. At the second, he heard the wood crack quietly. In that instant, he was aware of how she invited him and where, and it did not matter. There was a savage sweetness in her face, pain that she would cause him pain, happiness, blind and foolish, that called for him to come to her. If she saw anything, it was their life together—their *unlife*—children and lovers, wedded forever in the shadows.

Then his foot went through the rotten boards as, years later, most of his body would go through the rotted struts of a bridge.

The escaping maneuver was complex and almost hopeless, but somehow he achieved it, flinging himself away from the floor, and from her. He landed in the doorway in a shower of splinters. His head rang, and he heard her through the ringing, murmuring to him, coaxing him to return.

When he could look at her again, she was still smiling. She held out her hands, mutely encouraging him. A moment of discomfort, and all would be well. A moment, only a moment.

He staggered down the stair, and back into the school room. He was not certain what he meant to do, but, as if it had been planned, his confused gaze settled instantly on the tall wax time candle, and the flint and tinder that lay beside it.

He did not know—how could he?—that the ultimate act must be performed in their sight. Yet his instinct knew, that seventh sense which would make him what he was to become, that seventh sense which all that frightful day had been forming inside him, brain and soul.

When she drifted down the stair, he already had the candle alight. She glanced at it wonderingly, then took up a slate and a scrap of chalk. He was not amazed that she could hold them in her unreal hands, the shock came when she showed him what she had written. Not that he could read it. He would have needed a reflective surface for that. For, in the way of her kind, she had written unhesitatingly from right to left, back to front, in mirror writing. If he had needed any further sign, she had supplied it.

When he drew the packet of her hair from his belt, her eyes and mouth widened in frightful demented shapes. He had his first glimpse into hell, then, as the first of the great white moths dashed itself against him, throwing the filaments of its wings over his face, tearing him with the shards of its nails and its frantic unhuman eyes—

The burning packet of hair fell from the candle onto the tiles.

And as he destroyed her, in that minute he learned, and learned forever, that yes, it could be possible, and essential, and unbearably horrible, to kill the dead.

It was his very last lesson in that schoolroom, as it was his last night in that town or on that stretch of land.

When the rainwater, dripping through from above, quenched the smoldering ashes, he ran away into the undergrowth of night. He had been running from things since sunrise. Running from them, and toward them. Now too, he ran toward his future, and his trade. Although he did not know it, and just then would have wept if he had.

The fire was low. A crimson branch had broken open, whistling as the sap bled from it. The fortress wall hid the lights of the village from Parl Dro the man. Only the mild passage of the river at its summer low was audible, and sometimes a treacly chorus of frogs.

He was thinking the endlessly repeated question. *Did I simply curtail her dead-life because she would have robbed me of my human one?*

The answer came, as it always did, soothing him, never quite enough: He had not destroyed her in rage, not even merely in terror. He had grasped, or some part of him had, that this thing which would murder him, for whatever reason, could only be an echo, and a defiled echo at that, of the girl he had been companion to, the girl who had had such rights to love, whose human life he would have equated with his own. Wherever she had gone to, she had gone away from being that, that parody of herself.

The moon was up. A vixen screamed, miles off. He heard the muffled scrunch of a boot scraping on the brick causeway he had crossed hours earlier.

The imperative present had arrived.

Parl Dro sat, back to the wall, not moving. The meadow contained the footsteps which would now be negotiating it. Once there was a brief stumble. If he had not known, Dro might have taken it for some night beast tussling with rival or prey in the grass. Then the feet shambled over the uneven ground where the outer walls had come down. The stumbling was very evident now. Abruptly a voice cried out to him.

"Dro! Parl Dro! Are you here?"

Pitching his voice to carry as well, or better, than that cry, Dro said, "I'm here, Myal Lemyal."

The feet erupted into an uncertain gallop. Suddenly, around the wall, the musician careered into view. His face was dead white, his eyes appeared as black as Dro's. His hair streaked his forehead, plastered with sweat, and his sleeves flapped absurdly. Seeing Dro directly in front of him, he checked.

"So you're here."

"Unless, of course, you're imagining me."

Myal Lemyal jerked his head crazily. He drew the instrument off his shoulders and laid it carefully down. Then, with a hoarse bleak howl, he ran through the fire at Dro. There was a sharp stone in his right hand, the other was a stranglehold aimed for Dro's neck.

Dro came to his feet, lightly and without hesitation, as if both legs were whole and worked on springs. As Myal collided with him, Dro was no longer there. Myal hit the wall with a frustrated moan. Turning awkwardly, he made a clutch for Dro's sleeve. Dro allowed him to grab the sleeve. Myal raised the stone to smash it into Dro's face. The face was intent, yet somehow uninvolved. The stone dived forward and came away from Myal's hand uselessly. It whirred into the dark beyond the fire. They both heard it slam against another wall. The impetus of the abortive cast swung Myal over with it. He collapsed, tumbling against Dro, who caught him.

"I'll kill you," mumbled Myal, his head on Dro's shoulder. "You murdering bastard. I will. I'll kill you. I will."

"Of course you will."

Dro let him down gently to the ground. Myal sprawled there. He shook in uncontrollable waves of fury and fever, rolling almost into the fire. Dro rolled him back. Searing heat came through Myal's clothes. He was a furnace.

"I'll tear out your insides and tie them around your throat," the furnace said to him. "In a bow."

"How did you find me?"

"Don't know. I found you. I want to kill you. I came all this way to kill you. Why won't you come over here and let me do it? Damn you, I came all this way." Myal began to cry. "I can't do anything right, I never could." He buried his head in his arms. He cried as if his heart would shatter. Presently he said, "Don't beat me. Don't use the strap on me. Don't."

Dro pulled more branches across and piled them on the fire. The flames soared up, and Myal lay still on his side, watching them with the tears running sideways out of his eyes and into his hair.

"Next time," he said, "next time, I'll get it right. Don't hit me, Daddy."

"No one's going to hit you," Dro said.

"You will," Myal said, "I know you. You will, Daddy, when you've finished that skinful of beer."

Dro sat and looked at him. The shaking fit was gradually passing off. Myal stared at the fire, delirious, objective.

"It's easy to follow you," he said after a while. "You leave a kind of shadow behind you. I can't see it with my eyes, but I know it's there. I can find you simple as breath."

"In other words, you're gifted with powers beyond the normal."

"Lend me your knife," Myal said slowly. "I can kill you with it. It won't take a minute. I'll clean it after."

Myal's eyes shut. He sighed.

"You ought to be exterminated," he murmured. "I never had a big brother, someone to look up to. Someone I could kill."

"Go to sleep," Dro said.

"I wish I was dead."

"I wish you were, too."

Myal laughed.

"Did I ever tell you about the Gray Duke's daughter—?"

He slept, relaxed, comforted, across the fire from the man he had come to kill.

CHAPTER FIVE

The Gray Duke's daughter had made eyes at Myal. He had been flattered and afraid of her. She sidled up to him now with a wreath of lemon asphodel on her pale hair. Water ran out of her clothes and she was barefoot.

"Get up," she said, "you have only to walk twenty paces." Her voice was wrong. It was dark and clear and very definitely masculine.

"I don't want to get up," said Myal. "I don't want to walk."

"Yes you do," said the voice. The Duke's daughter had gone. Death, the King of Swords, was wrapping Myal in a blanket. The musical instrument was on Myal's shoulder and was being wrapped in the blanket too. Death was handsome, older by ten or twelve years, or maybe more, than Myal, and he had one scratched cheek. Women scratched. Down the back if they were in bed with you, on the face if they would not, or you would not, and they were angry.

"I see she got you then," said Myal conversationally, "marked you. I'm glad she did." He was not sure whom he meant. He was standing now but he had no legs. He was balanced on two columns of paper, which gradually buckled.

Death grasped him. They began to walk. "You won't get rid of me that easily," said Myal.

"I'm afraid I will."

They were in the open. An awful cold, or heat, smote Myal, disintegrating him. He fell forward dying, not caring that he died.

After a while, he was not dead. He was lying over the back of a small horse, watching the ground—high grasses, small stones, wild flowers—jog by between its hoofs. On the other side from his dangling face, upside down, two long black-booted legs walked, unevenly, and a black mantle swung.

"Where are we going?" asked Myal. He was having a lucid moment, he was fairly sure. He could tell the lucid moments, because they were the moments when he felt most ill. Yesterday—or had it been longer?—he had followed Parl Dro into the east. To start with, he had assumed Dro would stick to the road. Then, when Myal reached the track, he had been perplexed. It looked raw going for a lame man. On the other hand, the road ran off to the south. Stories of Ghyste Mortua tended to locate it east or north of east. By then, the itching, gnawing discomforts of Myal's body had turned into a bright blaze. Though his head ached, he felt intelligent and eager for some kind of action. His unformed fantasies of murdering Dro, gray and sickening before, had grown courageous, inspiring. He bolted off onto the track almost without thinking. After sunset, lost in the wood, he shouted at the trees. But Dro seemed to have left an imprint of his warped and blackened soul on them, which, as the fever worsened, slowly emerged.

When Myal saw the red spirit of the fire rising in a thin streamer from the fortress over the marsh, he picked up a sharp stone from the wayside. But something had gone wrong. Something always went wrong.

"Ciddey," he said to the ground.

"That's your reason, is it?" said the King of Swords.

Myal looked at the king's boots.

"She was very young to die," Myal said sentimentally. Tears ran out of his eyes. As each tear formed it blinded him, and then his sight returned as the drops dropped straight from the sockets onto the turf. One hit the upturned face of a flower. He could imagine it thinking: Ah! Now I have to contend with *salt* rain.

"If you'd just left them alone," Myal said. "She put her shoes on the bank. She fell back in the water. I tried to get to her, but when I got her out she was dead."

He abandoned himself once more to the fever. He lay, wrapped in misery, waiting for his consciousness mercifully to go out again. Then King Death was shaking him. Or seemed to be. The horse had stopped.

"What did you say?"

"What *did* I say? Don't know. You sure I said anything? Maybe just a delirious babble. You shouldn't take me too seriously—"

"Ciddey Soban. Are you telling me she's dead?"

"Oh," Myal yawned. Fresh tears dropped from his eyes. "She drowned herself. It was your fault, you damned bastard."

But something about Dro's voice, though quite flat, quite expressionless, brought Myal to the realization that of course the Ghost-Killer could not have known till now about Ciddey. It would have been stupid, after all, to slaughter a man for a crime he was unaware of having committed.

"With her sister gone, she had nothing left to live for," Myal explained.

Dro stood, looking away into the spaces of the morning. By twisting his head, Myal could see him, but it was too much of an effort to retain this position. Eventually Dro said,

"I'm glad for your sake your music isn't as trite as your dialogue."

The horse began to move again.

Myal sang the song he had made for Ciddey Soban, quietly, to the ground, until he fainted.

The hostelry was one of seven, but the only such place in the river village run by priests. The religious building stood off to one side, a whitewashed tower and wooden belfry piled on top of it. The hostel itself stood within a compound, a single long story of old brick. The priests came through a wicket gate into the compound to draw water at the well. Olive trees clawed in over the wall. There was a smell of the oil press, and of horses. Dro had hired the horse and the blanket from the priests. They were the only hospitalers in the district who would take in a sick man and care for him. Dro had been down at first light and found this out. And even the priests wanted paying. As he came through the dawn village and saw them, busy in their gardens and orchards, fishing in a pool, scurrying about with washing and baking, horses and dogs and cages of fowl, he wondered when, if ever, they made time to pray.

When he got back to the fortress, leading the horse for Myal, Myal was obviously too sick to travel over the meadow and the causeway and along the village street.

It was a sort of fever Dro had seen before, coming and going in tides. He waited for the next low tide, then hauled Myal into the meadow and shoveled him on the horse. It was almost noon by then.

Dro's plan had been straightforward. To offload the musician on the priests with enough cash to see ailment and convalescence out. That canceled all guilts, real or invented; Dro could return to his interrupted journey. That was the original plan. Myal's news altered things. If it were true. A delirious man might conjure innumerable dreams, believing each and all of them. But that was an insufficient blind. The sense in Parl Dro which judged such things had already credited the death of Ciddey Soban. Her death, and the ominous lacuna which followed it: the fact his premonitions had foreshadowed.

The holy brothers had a stretcher ready at the compound gate. Three of them lifted Myal and laid him on the stretcher and carried him into the single-story hostel.

Dro stood outside the open door, looking through into a room divided by wooden screens and shafts of sunlight. Bed frames were stacked in a corner. One bed had been prepared.

The color of the order was cream, the same color as the faded whitewashed walls. Everything blended, brick and linen and men, into a positively supernal luminescence. Myal might come to and think himself in some bizarre afterlife peopled by ugly angels.

One of the angels glided up to the man in black.

"An act of laudable charity, my son," said the priest, who was far younger than Dro. "To bring in the sick traveler and to pay for his lodging. Rest assured, your piety will not go unnoticed."

"Really? I thought I'd been fairly circumspect."

The priest smiled seriously.

"I think you mentioned moving on today. We might be able to come to some arrangement about a horse. Generally, of course, we don't buy and sell, but I'm sure we could agree on a price. Seeing your—er—your *difficulty*."

"What difficulty is that?"

The priest stared at him.

"Your affliction."

"Oh dear," said Dro, "have I been afflicted?"

"Your leg. I meant your lameness."

"Oh dear," said Dro, "you meant my lameness."

The priest went on staring, suddenly aware his point was being wilfully missed. He folded his hands in his sleeves, afraid their work-a-day calluses and gestures revealed too much.

"I'm certain you'd be better riding than walking about."

"Surely not inside the inn," said Dro.

He began to walk away, and the priest clicked his tongue at the limp. Dro stopped, turned and looked around at him. The priest involuntarily retreated a step and his hands fell back out of his sleeves.

Dro walked out of the compound and across the stepping stones in the water course, to the other side of the street. But striding past the open front of a leather worker's shop, he found the priest almost at his elbow again.

"My son, we must part as friends."

"I don't think it's obligatory, is it?"

"According to holy writ, it is," said the priest smugly. "All that meet as strangers should part as friends."

"Pity it's never caught on."

A woman leaned gracefully over a kiln where pots baked. Her hair was the color of the clay. She watched Dro intensely, lovingly. She touched a chord of memory he did not want, but the priest plucked his sleeve, distracting him.

"When you think about walking on, remember the horse. We can arrange it privately, if you wish. That way I can get you a reduction. Don't forget."

"My apologies," said Dro, "I seem to have forgotten."

He went through the door of the first inn.

The priest stood outside with his mouth drooping. When he turned, the red-haired woman had vanished from sight.

Twenty minutes later she came into the inn, voluptuous in a different dress, with copper leaves pendant from her ears.

The room was all but empty save for a cat or two and Parl Dro drinking the local wine in a corner.

She lifted a cup from the counter, crossed over to him and sat down facing him. He looked back at her silently.

"Aren't you going to offer me a drink?" she inquired.

"I'm not going to offer you a drink, but you can have a drink." He moved the flask toward her.

She filled the cup and drained it. Her skin was softly flushed by the sun. Her eyes were a foxy summer shade, catching flame from the metal leaves in her ears.

She said quietly: "My man's away." Dro sat and looked at her. "I mean," she said, "the house is empty. The bed's empty."

"No," he said. "Thank you."

"You don't like the look of me."

"The look of you is very appealing."

"But not to you."

"I'm the one who said it."

"But the one who doesn't want it. Or do I only remind you of someone else?" She smiled at him. "I'd like," she said, "to sail a boat across the black pools of your eyes. You're beautiful. Even better than they say. And much younger. I know who you are, you see. Maybe it's true, the other story." She waited for him to ask her what other story. Of course, he did not. She said, "The story no ghost-killer ever sleeps with anyone. That unspent sex builds up a reservoir of power. Like the proverbial virgin being able to snare a unicorn. Not that I'm saying you're a virgin. Or that there're unicorns, for that matter."

There was a silken dappling on the street. Silver strings tautened past the open door. The woman glanced at the rain.

"I think I know where you'll be going. If it exists. When you get there, you might wish you'd been nicer to me."

"Why?"

"Oh, you're interested now, are you? 'Why?' Because when I said my man was away, I was simplifying things. He left me two years ago, to try your business. He wasn't so clever, and didn't get so famous as you. I don't think he lived as long as you have, either. He left me to look for the old town, the one they call the Ghyste Mortua. He never came back. I never thought he would. Maybe he found some woman he liked better, and that's why he stayed away. Or maybe he

found the town, on the side of the hill, or in the lake, where
the landslide left it. The ghost town. And it killed him. He
could never make me understand. He said the Ghyste was in
this world, and not in it. That you could only find it at certain times of year, when particular stars were here, or there.
But he was one for the lusts of the flesh, my man. Perhaps
that's why he was no good at *your* vocation. Parl Dro."

She got up, turning her face to the rain flicker.

"This morning," she said, "awhile before sunrise, I saw a
girl go up the street. There was no one else about. She went
right by under my window. I didn't recognize her, but it was
dark still. Then I saw something shining. She was leaving wet
footprints on the street. She went toward the priests' hostelry.
When she got close to the wall of the compound, the first
light started to come, and I could see the brickwork right
through her back."

The woman stood looking at the rain.

Presently he spoke.

"Maybe you should alter your trade."

"Maybe I have. I played the riddle-blocks later. I cast the
King of Swords, that's you. And in the Zodiac, the water sign
of the Two Fish, and the air sign of the Harp—that'd be your
sick friend, probably—the sign of the weakling and the genius.
She was there, too. The Virgin, riding on the unicorn, gripping the chain around his neck. Watch out, handsome hero."

"All right," he said. "Thanks for the warning."

"If you want me," she said, "for anything, it's the house
behind the potter's shop. I'm called Cinnabar."

"I'll remember."

"See you do."

During the afternoon, when smooth rain shadows slicked
the hostel, Myal's fever had lifted him on firework wings. He
had chattered at great length, and one by one the priests had
stolen in to listen. They heard quite a few unusual things as,
under the pretense of stoking the brazier, bringing fresh
coals, blankets, aromatics and wet cloths to moisten the story-
teller's burning lips, they clustered at the bedside.

They heard of strange predilections of the Cold Earl's, of
moonlight falling on naked maidens astride the backs of stal-
lions. They learned of the Gray Duke's daughter, and a certain sequence in a wood. They learned of court orgies and

romps. And sad seasons when leaves ran yellow in the streams and money came in the shape of other men's pockets. They learned of Myal's drunken father, bloody-eyed and strap in fist, and of all the bullies who had assumed that father's shape in later years, dukes, innkeepers, stewards and jailers. The priests clotted close to Myal as ants on honey. They gaped and gasped, and held their breaths and squeaked. As they were thrashed with Myal, and seduced with Myal, and chased with Myal. As they cowered and thieved and played music and made love and lay in the corners of prisons with Myal.

As the dark day thickened and declined, they sagged feebly all about the sick bed, almost dead of second-hand living.

Then a break came in the western overcast, and a ray of low amber sun sheered through a window. Exactly on this cue, Myal's tidal fever smashed itself to pieces on some high and fiery shore. With a sudden sigh, he dropped still and dumb on the mattress, every muscle relaxed, his breathing soft and rhythmic as a low quiet song. A song without words.

The brothers shook themselves dolefully. They praised a higher authority, in disappointed voices, for the traveler's cure. All but one, duty-bound to remain, hurried away.

The last priest dozed, dreaming of dinner, which gradually became dinner in the Cold Earl's hall. A naughty girl on a black horse cantered up the room, throwing flowers and fruits to the diners. When she reached the priest, she threw a furious jailer, brandishing a leather belt, into his lap.

The priest woke with a start.

It was dark, the sun down and the windows deep blue. He was about to rise and light the candles when he felt again the extraordinary sensation of a separate live entity on his knee. Not a brutish jailer, certainly, it was too light. He chuckled to himself, thinking one of the puppies had strayed into the hostel. He put out his hand gently to pat the beast—and encountered a cool scaly flapping.

With a yelp, the priest started up, overturning his chair. As he did so, a beam of light, falling across the room from the half-open door and the refectory beyond the compound, caught a vague pale swirling in the area of the traveler's bed. It was rather like smoke, more like water, and in the midst of it something slowly turned and floated.

The priest felt a horrible drawing sensation like faintness, and he became icy cold.

Somehow he tottered to the door and out of it. He had no thought for his patient, indeed few thoughts at all until he staggered into the lamp-lit refectory.

The inn was filling up with evening trade. The Ghost-Killer was seated on a bench in a corner. He had eaten frugally half an hour before sunset. The flask of wine was two-thirds full and stoppered. He was drinking water when the two priests hurried in.

Everyone looked. Though all the priests drank heartily, they did not do it in the sinful public house.

More interesting yet was the way the brothers rushed immediately to the stranger in the black mantle.

"Answer me," cried the fatter of the two priests—both were reasonably fat—"Are you the man we reckon you to be?"

"Let's start again," said Dro lazily. "Who do you think I am?"

"One of those lawless and unholy—" rattled off the lesser fat priest.

The other swiped him. "Be quiet, you fool." He added to Dro: "We reckon you to be one skilled in the exorcism of undead spirits."

Dro watched them.

"And so?"

The fatter priest contained his dignity. "And so, we require your services, my son."

The room eyed them, ears pinned back. Even the row of cats, perched in the beer barrels, listened, wide-eyed.

"The fact is, my son," said the lesser fat priest, unbending from his distaste, "we're probably mistaken, but—"

"But we've had a strange occurrence in the hostelry where your friend is being nursed. We feel that you owe us some responsibility, my son."

"I concede," said Dro, "that one of you may have got out over the wall some night. But to accept both of you as fathers would be biologically unsound. Besides, I think the woman misled you. Try a little arithmetic. I'd say I was unlikely to be the son of either of you, unless you conducted a courtship prior to the womb."

The room in general made a little explosive crowing noise. Both priests changed color. The lesser snapped,

"He's a rogue and a devil. Leave him alone. The idiot brother in the hostel was half asleep. Here we are, letting ourselves and our habit be insulted, just because some imbecile dreamed there was a live fish in his lap." He flung about, glaring at the room and its inadequately suppressed laughter. He jumped when Parl Dro walked past him and out of the door.

Scrambling the same way, the two priests observed Dro crossing the street by the stepping stones and going around the wall and through into the compound. They hurried after him. In groups, drinkers from the inn began to follow, halting however at the compound gate.

That stretch of street, and the space before the religious building and its subsidiary architecture, grew bright and cherry with struck tinders, drink and shouted inquiry. Crowd attracted crowd. A hundred persons soon blocked the thoroughfare. Priests swarmed like cream bees back and forth, ordering the crowd, as they struggled through it, into temporary areas of silence. No direct information was supplied, but fragment by fragment the tale grew. There was a ghost in the hostel.

The priests kept their distance from the hostel door, staying actually outside the compound, as the crowd had done. Parl Dro had paused in the compound of necessity, since the brotherhood had nervously barricaded the hostel door with logs, posts and baskets—as if a ghost would normally fear to pass straight through such domestic trivia. Dro tossed and thrust these items aside, then crashed open the door, crashing it shut again as soon as he was inside.

The hostel was black now, with black starless cavities of windows. Picking up the priest's toppled chair, Dro slung it against the door timbers, a barricade with a new purpose—to keep any other live thing out.

The room was cold and dripping—dank as someone's dungeon.

At first, there was nothing else, except that the racket of the swelling crowd in the street seemed unduly muffled and far away.

Dro's eyes dilated to pierce the gloom. Soon, he was seeing well, via the cat-sight of the extra seventh sense. He did not touch the candles or the tinder box. Now and then a dart of light from the host of tinders outside would streak over the wall. But slowly, the brightness of these darts grew dull. Then he began to hear the melodious winnowing of sound, the sound of the stream below the mountain. Cilny's stream. And Ciddey's.

Myal, whom the priests had courageously abandoned— more, trapped inside with the unknown terror—had remained oblivious. He lay on the bed, peacefully slumbering. It was a peace that filled Parl Dro with iron rage.

Dro took one stride forward, but in that second, the manifestation began to return.

She formed, little by little, in the shade just over the far edge of Myal's bed. She was visible from the knees upward, and below her knees, across the mattress and Myal's body, flowed the smoky convolutions of the water. She was mainly transparent. Even so, Dro could see she showed none of the rigors of drowning, though plainly, if unconsciously, she recollected exactly how she had died. Her face was calm and empty at first, but as she looked at him, focused on him, her face altered. Her eyes seemed to sink and to enlarge into mere sockets. She grinned, and her grin was terrible, unspeakable, showing only her lower teeth. She raised her hands, and she held a freshwater fish in them. She bore it to her mouth as if to kiss it, then sank her teeth into its squirming living back. A trickle of pallidly gleaming blood ran down her chin.

It was an illusion, the fish. She was even more a witch, dead, than she had been alive. She fashioned such forms to intimidate him. When she perceived he was not intimidated, the fish, the trickle of blood, even the swirl of the ghostly stream evaporated.

She hung there, still smiling vilely at him. Then her smile went away, and she too slid away, back and back and back, as the inescapable force of Dro's will pushed her.

She opened her mouth in a soundless cry, and lifted her hands again. Her nails were already very long. She fought him, but he was used to such fighting, and she was not. He thrust her all the way to the wall, seeming to press her, like a phosphorescent imprint, into the whitewash. Her hair blew or fanned out like a misty colorless sunburst—moonburst—on the bricks. He held her pinned like that, and then, never taking his eyes from her, he fastened one pitiless hand over

Myal's throat, squeezing the windpipe until, gagging and choking, the musician flailed into consciousness.

Dro unfastened the stranglehold. Myal croaked a number of expletives and accusations. Dro cut him short, dragging Myal's head around by the hair toward the wall.

"*Look.*"

Myal froze, petrified, rigid as a stone in Dro's grip.

"What—what is it?"

"Don't you know?"

"Ciddey—it's Cidd—"

"Don't keep naming her. She has enough of a hold on you as it is. How do you feel?"

"I feel sick." A ludicrous note of reproach crept into Myal's voice. "I haven't been well."

"You'll be less well if she goes on feeding off you."

"Feeding—"

"She's using your life energy to supplement her own. Can't you feel it?"

"I. . . . Something. I feel terrible."

Dro let him fall back on the mattress. Dro never once let his own eyes slip from the apparition, stapled like a moth to the wall. Even as he spoke, three quarters of his mind and a great deal of his strength were being utilized to keep her as far from her life source, Myal, as possible. To prevent her, also, from flight. For she might come to see that flight was her only current ploy.

"What did you bring with you, Myal," Dro said, "from the stream?"

"*What?*"

"The stream where she died. You took something from her body. A lock of hair, a ribbon—*something.*"

"*No.*"

"Don't conceal it. It's her link. Look at her. She'll kill you, one way or another. Either persuade you to die to appease her jealousy of your life. Or draw your life out of you, moment by moment."

"I think," said Myal. He coughed. "I think I brought one of her shoes. I don't know why. I forgot I had. They were cloth, very small. I trod on one on the bank. I was already getting sick. Didn't know what I was—"

"Where?"

"The instrument. Where is it? Somebody must have put it somewhere."

"It's there by the bed. Reach over and hand it to me."

"I can't. I'm too weak to move."

"You'll move."

"All right—I'll—try—"

Myal floundered around. His arms were trembling so much he could hardly get hold of the sling, but he managed it, and lugged the grotesquerie of wood and strings onto the mattress. To touch it steadied him. But the shoe, crumpled together, had been shoved into the opening over the sound box, and through into the hole of the instrument. Invisible. He could not remember doing this. Yet, somehow, he could. . . .

Still not looking at him, Dro tore the shoe out of Myal's hand.

"Whatever happens now, stay where you are, and stay quiet."

"What's liable to happen?"

Myal cringed and shot a glance at the blocked door. But his head swam. He flopped on his face, hiding his eyes.

Parl Dro stood midway between the bed and the door. He dropped the little shoe on the ground. The sole had cracked where Myal had palmed it into a ball. Pathetic, desolate little shoe.

Dro took the tinder from his shirt and struck a flame. At the rasp of flint and fire, Myal burrowed more deeply in the bolster. Dro stooped, awkward from the crippled leg, and set the shoe alight, bracing himself as he did so for the ghost's dying frenzy. Which did not come.

As the flame fluttered around the shoe, destroyed it, and expired on the flags, Dro stared at what was left of Ciddey Soban, plastered, insectile and beautiful, on the wall. She never moved. With vast extinguished eyes, she gazed at him. And then she melted like frost. And she was gone.

The dungeon chill swilled instantly off the room and down some supernatural drain.

Parl Dro drew a deep breath. The familiar exhaustion clambered on his back, dragged him down. Exhaustion, and something else. Something—something—

Outside, the noise of the crowd had mounted, now the eerie barriers were gone from the air. Footsteps ran across the compound, and the door rocked to blows. There had been enough people in the street, and concentrating hard enough, to form a kind of composite pseudo seventh sense. Sufficient to guess when the exorcism was complete.

He pulled the chair away from the door.

Myal groaned. "Is it over? Whatever it was?"

"I hope it is." Dro checked, hand on the door, appalled by what he had just said. Never before had there been any doubt.

CHAPTER SIX

The drinking party went on into the small hours.

Most of the village had heard, many had been spectators. Spectators who had actually *seen* nothing, only felt, and half understood. The priests filed solemnly through the hostel, now it was safe, blessing it and sprinkling unguents. They blessed and sprinkled Myal, too. Pale and shaking, clinging to the sling of the instrument, he said to Parl Dro: "I'm sorry." "You're not only sorry, you're a damn fool," said Dro. He had walked out into the night and the village had borne him away to an accompaniment of shouts and clanking flasks. He was too tired to resist. No, it was not that he was so tired. He wanted to drown something, worse than nagging pain, a nagging doubt. So he sat with the village and tried to get drunk, while they tried to get uncanny anecdotes out of him. Mainly he fended them off; they fell to recounting their own ghost stories—factual or imaginary. They told him the fortress on the meadow was haunted. When he said he had slept there the previous night, they exchanged wise looks. He knew better than to attempt convincing them there had been no haunt in the fortress. No one without the seventh sense could normally tell ghost from brick.

A few hours later, most of them were sprawled in various stages of stupor. Dro was still sober, though his nerves hummed quietly, as if they felt they should, from the alcohol in his blood.

He went out of the inn and down the street in the star-slit darkness, to clear his head, or to make believe that it needed clearing. While he could pretend he was a little drunk, he could partake of the drunkard's privilege and not think.

The rain clouds were gone. The moon was leisurely sliding down the slope to the belfrey.

The woman called Cinnabar sat at the front of the potter's shop. Queen of Fires. A dull glow lingered in the eye of the kiln, and she was in its way, catching the light on cheek and breast and hair, and on her moving hands. She was pinching out a little clay dog by moonlight. She glanced up and saw Parl Dro standing by the unlocked gate, watching her.

"You look tired to death," she said.

"Aren't we all."

"Sometimes."

"Can I come inside?" he said.

She looked down, almost shyly.

"Didn't I say you could."

He stepped into the shop. It smelled of baked clay, and of some warm subtle perfume she was wearing. He had not noticed it on her before.

"I'll offer you my bed again," she said to the dog. "This time, just to sleep in. It's a rare bed. Feather mattress deeper than sixteen seas piled one on the other. It'll do you good. You look properly done up. But I remind you of someone, don't I?"

He stood by her. Her fingers were very agile with the dog. It looked quite real, almost familiar, as if it might wag its tail, cock a leg or bark at any minute. He leaned down and gently kissed her temple. Her hair had a gold edging from the fire, and the marvelous scent came from her hair.

"You're very talented, Cinnabar," he said, "and you have a beautiful smell."

Her fingers left the dog.

"My man gave me a comb from some foreign place. The scent's in the wood, and when I comb my hair, my hair takes the scent, too."

"I'm sorry you lost him," he said.

"You're not," she said. She rose and turned and looked at him. Her eyes were bright with tears. "Or maybe you are. I'm ashamed of myself," she said. "Making up to a stranger. Or am I a stranger to you? Am I so very like her?"

"You'd prefer me to go."

"No," she said. "The beds at the inn are full of vermin."

"Perhaps suitable company."

"Oh, you," she said. Her tears seeped away again into their fount.

He kissed her in a rich dark forest of hair. The unique comfort of human flesh bound both of them tightly together for some while after the kiss had finished.

"Tomorrow, before you leave," she said, "there's something—I'll tell you. Is your companion well enough to travel?"

"What companion?"

"The boy at the hostel. The man the ghost was visiting."

"He's nothing to me."

"Ah," she whispered, "don't be too sure."

She kissed him this time, smoothing his hair in long, repeated, serene and sensuous caresses. Presently she took his hand, and led him up the little stair, along the passageway, and into the feather bed sixteen seas deep.

The strains of music spearing out of the hostel door were wonderful to the extent almost of sorcery. They fell in the compound in shards, like the morning sunlight. Pigeons paraded, cooing in bemused fascination. A cat lay not far off, eyes narrowed, belly tilted to the sun, apparently a music lover and not hungry.

As he made the music, a sense of glorious well-being invaded the musician. When he left off, high waters of debility swept back in on him. Panting and dizzy, he set the instrument aside and curled on the bed. Silence. A cat leaped past the door, and the pigeons leaped into the air. A woman with terra-cotta hair came over the threshold.

Myal looked at her uneasily. Most women intrigued and scared him. Quite a few men too, for that matter. But then he relaxed. The woman had a sweet and satiated look. Her heart belonged somewhere that was not here. She was totally unobtainable: safe.

"You've a great knack with music," she said.

"Oh, thank you." Myal smiled modestly.

"Parl Dro," said the woman, "left the village an hour before sunup."

Myal's face flattened with dismay. He sat up, went white, and lay down again.

"That's that then."

"Not necessarily. If you were fit to travel by tomorrow."

"I won't be, anyway. Anyway, I can't catch him up again. Anyway, what's in it for you?"

He could guess what *had* been in it for her. So this was the type that attracted King Death. Very nice too. But why was she interested in Myal?

"I read the blocks. They showed the two of you. There's a balance that needs you both."

"Did he tell you about—"

"Ghyste Mortua? I know about it. I have reason to bear a grudge against the deadalive in that place."

"It's all a story," said Myal slyly.

"Like the thing in here last night?"

Myal involuntarily glanced behind him. Despite the unguents of the priests, despite the exorcism, he had not slept easily in this room. Only illness had let him sleep at all, drugging him with inertia.

"Well, a *good* story. Maybe true."

"There was a town," she said, low, staring at him, seeing not him, but images in her mind. Myal, lying dizzily watching her, began to see them too.

The name of the town had been Tulotef. It stood on the side of a tall hill, above a valley where a wide river ended in a curious star-shaped lake with four subsidiary stretching channels. Forest bloomed over the uplands. Distant crags, pale as winter, towered from the trees. The ways to Tulotef were limited and occult. It was, besides, a town good to itself alone. Other towns it had greeted with swords and fusillades; retaliatory armies came to have the boiling juice of almonds and olives dashed on their heads. The walls of Tulotef, sloping, slaty, crenellated, might be opened only voluntarily and only where there were gates. Those within were declared to be witches. From the highest to the lowest, all had some smattering of spells, and many, a large compendium. That was the legend. The vernacular said: *When we dance in Tulotef.* Which meant: *Never.* Then something did get into Tulotef, something did bring it down, towers, roofs, walls, gates. One summer night, there was an earth-tremor, not in itself unheard of, nor in itself disastrous. But there was, so the tale went, a fault that ran around the upper gallery of the hill on the side of which Tulotef was built. Unseen, the fault had lain in wait, weathering the sun, the snow, the wind, and all the shocks of the earth, for hundreds of years, like a dragon under water. Then came this ultimate tremor, slight in itself, which sliced through the last hair-fine joists that remained to hold the hill. Not long past midnight, when the town was loud with bells and processions and feasts for some occasion sacred to itself, the watchmen spied a vast black bird that lifted from the hilltop, spreading enormous wings.

To picture the moment was not hard. The sudden cessation of all sound, the lifted heads, raised faces, pointing hands, all in the glitter of lamps and candles, the dying notes of bells, the sparkle of ornaments and eyes. Then the gigantic thunder, the unconscionable geographic growl, as the top of the hill snapped off, disintegrated, burst. A rain of particles, boulders, rubble crashed on Tulotef. Onto the screaming faces, dainty fires. Then the inexorable tons of granite and stone and streaming earth itself, marched down the hill against the city. It was the last army. It gushed like a tidal wave against the walls and broke them, the gates and splintered them. It rolled through the town and the town was gone, its life crushed and its fires put out. And then, a huge burial mound, the town itself began to move. It slipped from its foundations, and fell away down the hill into the star-shaped lake.

Not one living thing survived.

And yet, if the legend were a fact, all had survived. In a way. Now the spot was called Ghyste Mortua, for on particular nights the dead came back to the void where Tulotef had been, some thousands of witch-gifted, hating, evil ghosts. And in the lake below, held pristine and inviolate, their linkage to the world, every link they could desire; their treasures, their bones, the bricks and mortar of their town.

They abducted the living, enticed the living, fed from them, slew them. They tore up graves, they worked spells. The very land stank of wickedness.

If any of it was true.

"I know this," said the red-haired woman, "whoever goes that way, never comes back."

"Rather stupid to go there then," remarked Myal. His hands trembled, though it was really only what he had heard before.

"Parl Dro is going there. And you."

"*Me*? You're joking. I wouldn't be seen dead there. Oh. What I mean is—"

"It's a compulsion. I know. I've seen it before. There's always a reason you find for yourself, an excuse—a legend to prove or disprove, a battle to engage, a poem or a song to create—but it's the place itself, issuing a challenge. A war game. It used to call armies to fight it. Now it calls certain men. At certain times. Certain women, too."

"You're not—" said Myal.

"Not me."

Myal pulled the musical instrument to him by the sling and put his arms around the wooden body.

"I knew," she said, "he would leave today, before he knew it. And you'll leave tomorrow. You owe him a debt, don't you? He paid the priests for your care."

"I owe him a knife in the ribs," said Myal.

The woman laughed. Myal glanced at her in astonishment.

"Rest well," she said. "Tomorrow at first light I'll bring you a horse. Not one of the priests' horses, but my own. I'll set you on the way as well; I know the start of it. You'd probably find him anyhow, but to be sure. If you give the horse her head, you'll catch up to him before tomorrow's sunset."

"I can't afford a horse," said Myal.

"I'm not selling a horse. When you reach him, you must let her graze a while, then turn her and send her back to me. She knows the way, too."

"I can't afford to hire a horse, either," said Myal pompously. He held the instrument as tightly as if someone were trying to drag it away from him. His arms quivered with the tension.

"No fee, no hire. A loan."

"What's the snag?"

"You're very suspicious."

"I've learned to be."

"Then unlearn it."

She smiled at him. Her smile was like a ray of sun. She went out.

He lay stiff as a knotted twig, for about an hour, terrified of everything, and of himself. Then the terror went off. Securely alone, he bragged to himself. The woman liked him after all. She wanted to help him because she fancied him. As for Dro, who could be so useful being so famous, Myal could get around him. As for Ghyste Mortua, that was just a wild romantic fantasy, the sort a minstrel had to have, had to pretend to believe in. And the wonderful song he would make of the ghostly town, its shriveled towers, the greenish fireflies spinning in its endless dusks—the song was already partly formed in his head, his fingers. The quest was all he needed. To travel hopefully. Certainly, *not* to arrive.

He dozed, and woke at early evening to the priests' supper bell. No one had bothered to bring him anything to eat, but he felt fine. Fit and self-assured.

He swaggered over to the refectory and strode in on long, reasonably steady legs.

The priests looked up nervously, their pudgy faces bulging with food.

Myal sauntered along the tables, tore off a wing of roast chicken, took up a brimming mug of yellow cider.

"Really, my son," they remonstrated, "guests do not eat in the refectory."

"This was paid for, wasn't it," Myal demanded, frowning at them, "by my friend Parl? Before he had to go on ahead of me. Pass me that loaf. And the salt."

He caught a glimpse of himself in a polished ewer. He had moved abruptly into one of his handsome phases. His hair was burnished, his features were chiseled. He looked just like the prince he had always known he really was. That man with the strap—how could that thing have been the genetic father of Myal?

Myal lounged in a chair. He had some ham, ordered a bath. He stole three purses out of two habits.

In the middle of the night, happily bleary from a soak in hot water and a liver soaked in cider, he wandered back across the compound for the purposes of nature. Then, with a sense of his own ridiculous generosity, he returned the purses, though not exactly into their owners' pockets. He threw them instead nimbly on the compost heap, at its jammiest section.

He woke feeling virtuous and well. Even the cider had not gone sour on him.

He took the instrument, went to the well, drew some water and splashed around in the bucket for a while. When he looked up, the sky was lifting into light, and the red-haired woman stood at the gate. He knew her name by then. He had asked one of the priests. The priest had been shocked. Simply saying a woman's name had seemed to shock him.

She came across the compound, and gave Myal an apple. The immemorial symbol did not alarm him. It would have, if it had not been her. He ate the apple, enjoying it, though the Gray Duke's daughter had once insisted he and she simultaneously devour an apple hung by cord from a rafter. It had been a rough enterprise. Their teeth had clashed once or twice and he had been afraid of being bitten. It was a forfeit. Whoever ate least of the apple lost. Myal lost. If he had won, the punishment would actually have been the same.

But he was at ease with Cinnabar. She must admire him very much, but apparently chastely, wanting nothing.

Outside the compound, a roan mare stood docilely. He had not ridden in months, years, but the mare had a tender pretty face. He liked her at once, and shared the last of the apple with her lovingly.

When he was mounted, the instrument on his shoulders, Cinnabar showed him a bag of provisions tied to one side of the saddle.

"You can keep that. But send my horse back to me."

"Of course I will," he said very sincerely.

Cinnabar took his hand and placed in it an amazing little clay dog. It looked so realistic, Myal laughed. It was still faintly warm from the firing. He gazed at Cinnabar, and swallowed. Whenever anyone gave him anything, truly *gave* it, he was emotionally, almost agonizingly, touched.

"Go on," she said. She was crying slightly, and smiling at him. Myal, also crying a little and grinning foolishly, nodded several times, and tapped the mare.

She took off at a mercurial gallop that surprised and almost unseated him.

After he got used to the savage galloping of the roan mare and they were far from the village, Myal recalled Cinnabar had offered him no directions. That he had found Dro previously was evidence of Myal's brilliant powers of deduction. But now he ran blind, or the horse did. Then it occurred to him that Cinnabar had told him that the horse knew the road. When he considered it, their direction seemed correct, for they plunged toward the rising sun.

At first, there were tracks running parallel along the loop of the river, then veering away.

Low hills flowed up from the land to the left. On the right hand the river plain spread into limitless distances, shining transparently in the young morning, through a soft powder of mist.

Then a wood swept down on horse and rider. River and hills and tracks were gone.

Leaves whipped by. Birds flirted across Myal's face. The horse slowed, and began to pick her way at a fast delicate trot.

Myal was struck by a picture of himself.

He brought the instrument around on its sling and rested it on his chest. The rough material of the sling, the scrawls of paint on the wood and the uneven chips of ivory sunk in it excited him with a still, reassuring excitement. The bite of the wires into the old calluses on his fingers filled him with a wild pure wave of peace. He improvised, using the strings only, a dance for the horse.

Sometimes he marveled when he thought about the complexity of the instrument. It was so simple to him, yet who else on earth would ever be able to play it? Two only that he knew of, its inventor, and the strap-brandishing father—who had never properly mastered it. Myal watched his fingers curiously. The secret lay in some mysterious affinity between prediction, inner ear and action. Each touch on any string of one neck supplied not only a note, but the pressure to tune in the note on the opposite neck—which supplied, vice versa, its own note and simultaneous pressure for the first note. When the reed was blown, the fingers that caused these pressures, coincidentally stopped the various holes, activating in turn other notes. But how could one man carry three or more opposing harmonies, all interrelating, dependent upon each other, in his brain at once. In fact, when Myal played the entire assemblage of the instrument at once, six or seven or even eight lines of melody could emanate from it, chords, descants and contrapuntal fugues.

The mare liked the music.

Sunlight rained through the leaves.

He stayed in the saddle until they came out of the wood on a rocky slope up in the air.

A huge landscape sprawled away on all sides. He was high enough to observe the strange natural quarterings of the land, divided like a board game by dim smoke lines of trees, the slashes of ravines, troughs of valleys. The river, a last partition, spilled to the south, slender as a tear. There were no roads that Myal could see. Dismounted, he peered down the craggy slope.

"Lost the way yet?" he asked the horse.

She pulled forward against the reins.

When they reached the bottom of the slope, he found they were in a dry stream bed, and went on leading her over littered pebbles and moss. The stream opened out, just after noon, into a park-like flatness with the trees elegantly poised at intervals in courtly groups. He investigated the provision bag and ate. The horse neatly clipped the grass, gardening restfully.

They rode on at a medium pace over nearly flat ground, which still sloped at an infinitesimal angle downward. The walls of rocky hills ran alongside northeast and south, but miles off. Great clouds swam over, like the keels of enormous ships in the sky. The afternoon became full-blown, and one by one its petals started to drop away.

Myal saw Dro suddenly conjured before him, walking, a tiny black figure, like a speck, then a beetle.

Myal's reaction was reflexive. He pulled on the reins and the mare halted. Myal shivered, his stomach turned over and sank, all of which annoyed him. He tapped the horse, and she broke into a whirlwind sprint.

If Dro heard him coming, which seemed likely, he did not look around or even bother to get out of the way.

Myal raced past him in a spray of speed and kicked-up clods. He wheeled the mare about and stopped her in Dro's path. Myal raised his brows and stared at Dro in the midst of the wide and uninhabited land.

"Well, *fancy* meeting you."

CHAPTER SEVEN

"Where did you steal the horse?"

Dro had given no evidence of any particular reaction, and his voice was noncommittal.

Myal sat in the saddle, suddenly depressed.

"I didn't steal it. It's on loan from your girl friend."

Dro said nothing.

Myal began to feel tired and weak. He remembered he had been delirious with fever only two days ago, and a wave of shocked self-pity swept over him.

"It wasn't my idea," said Myal, "to follow you. Your red-head persuaded me. She seemed to think you might need me."

Dro laughed, short and sharp.

"All right," said Myal. "Screamingly funny."

He slid off the horse and stroked her dejectedly. She lowered her head and bit at the grass. The light was solidifying, fragrant with currents of wind that tasted of clover or trees. The imminent end of day brought to Myal an imperative desire to communicate. He looked at Dro.

"I have to send the horse back to the village."

"Why not go back with her?"

"I told you. I'm heading for Ghyste Mortua. Just like you."

Dro made a briefly theatrical sweeping gesture to the east, offering Myal the freedom of the nonexistent road: "Please."

"Put it this way," said Myal desperately. "I owe you some money. Debts worry me." He broke off. He wondered why he was so desperate. Probably it was a simple fear of being left alone by night in this weirdly self-sufficient open country, no trace of a human presence anywhere, save here.

"I release you from your debt," said Dro. He walked by Myal and away.

Myal stood and stared after him, struggling for arguments, and against his own absurd panic. The black figure grew small again, and smaller, and the light reddened. Myal glanced westward. The sun had lowered in a group of trees. The trees were on fire, but did not burn, and inch by inch, the sun slipped through the bottom of their cage of branches.

Dro was about two hundred yards away.

The mare had shifted her ground. Myal called to her, and she turned to gaze at him. In the copper light, she too was made of copper. When he called again and took a step in her direction, she tossed her head, kicked up her heels and bounded off, back the way they had come. In half a minute, she had vanished behind stands of trees. Possibly she had taken his yell as the homeward instruction, but to Myal it looked more like sheer perversity. The bag of provisions was still firmly tied to her saddle. Myal turned and looked at Parl Dro, small now as a black beetle again. Myal began to run after him, on legs that were uncertain and stiff from riding. His head sang. When Dro had grown back to the height of Myal's hand, Myal decelerated into a shaky stride.

Presently Dro looked over his shoulder. He looked, and looked away, keeping moving. Myal put on another enforced burst of speed. The instrument thumped him on the back, as if encouraging him. Then either Dro had slowed his pace or Myal increased his beyond the speed he thought himself capable of, for abruptly he caught up to Dro, and they were walking alongside each other.

"Don't mind me," said Myal airily. "I just happen to be going the same way as you."

"So I see."

"The bloody horse ran off. All the bloody food was in a

bloody bag tied on the bloody saddle. That's bloody well gone too."

Dro walked. Myal glanced at him and away.

"This seems quite a nice spot to bivouac for the night."

"So bivouac."

"Don't you think," said Myal, "we should stick together? There could be a lot of big animals about in a place like this after dark. Two of us together would stand a better chance of—fighting anything off."

Dro walked. Myal set himself to the task of simply keeping up. The lame stride was powerful and set its own decided rhythm.

Side by side, unspeaking, they moved over the wild park, and the light closed like a door behind them.

Darkness swirled from the thickets, the trees, from pockets in the ground. The sky, a smooth sheet of dark lavender, put out a thousand stars.

There was a sudden break in the landscape. Around a wall of silent folded poplars, the earth tipped over into one more ravine, this time very shallow, some seven yards deep at most, about five feet across. A dense stream of night was already flowing there. On the far side, a bare humped hill ascended, with one towering oak tree flung up from it in a pagoda of leaves.

There was a thin noise of water, not in the ravine, but to one side, along the edge. A spring flickered from the rock and over, uselessly, into the gully.

Dro crossed to the spring and kneeled, presumably drinking or filling a flask; in the gathering dark it was hard to see. When Dro moved away and began to set a fire between the poplars, Myal went to the spring in turn and drank. Then he moved across to watch Dro. The fire was economically constructed. It made use of a natural scoop in the earth, a few stones to contain and conduct the heat, dry twigs for the base, those less dry set near to cook out moss or rain before being added.

"You're very good," said Myal admiringly.

Dro lit the fire and sat, his back against a poplar trunk, his hood pushed off. That shadowy king's face, gilded by flame, intimidated Myal, who stood awkwardly, as if waiting to be asked to sit down. Without warning, Dro's glowing black eyes fixed on him. The stare was profound, hypnotic, ruthless and inimical. Myal writhed under it, then snapped like one of the twigs.

"So this is the end of our beautiful friendship, is it? You really think I'm that much of a dead loss, do you?"

Dro's eyes never moved, did not even blink. Just his mouth said, "I really think you are."

"In that case, I'm off." Myal added sarcastically, "I know when I'm not wanted."

"Your life must be a series of departures."

Raging and impotent, Myal turned on his heel and walked straight into a tree.

Having disengaged himself, he strode away along the side of the ravine, far enough to be out of Dro's sight. He lay down where a boulder provided partial shelter and a partly reassuring anchor at his spine. He hugged the instrument and curled himself together around it. The earth was growing cold and magnetically still.

He lay like that some while, feeling alone and dwarfed under the wide night, inventing cutting rejoinders to Parl Dro's comments, blaming his own status and person for all the ills life had showered on him.

He fell asleep and dreamed Cinnabar's clay dog had got out of his pocket and was barking and frisking in the meadow, until one of its jumps broke it on a stone. Red blood flowed from the clay and Myal wept in his sleep. For comfort, his dream hands closed on wire strings and began to play them. It was the song he had made for Ciddey Soban.

Any compunction Parl Dro might have felt was inevitably tempered by the realization that the crazy minstrel was even now probably less than a hundred feet off. Not that Dro was particularly inclined to compunction. From thirteen until he was fifteen, he had worked his way up and down various tracts of land, now as herder, now as farmhand, now as escort for or carrier of trade goods, and he had learned his own methods of survival. Myal Lemyal, from the look of things, had had a life as rough, dangerous and soul-destroying. His methods of survival were not Parl Dro's, yet they were methods and he had survived. Dro had more respect for Myal's abilities than Myal could guess. And less time for him than even Myal's paranoia intimated. It was not aversion exactly, but simply that Dro's singularity had grown to be a habit. He would break from it for a day, a night, now and then. But he was used to being companionless. Used to himself as seen only through his own implacable eyes.

At fifteen, when he was still capable of becoming reasonably gregarious, and exceedingly drunk, Parl Dro had accepted a bet, for a pound bag of silver, to sleep the night in a haunted barn. At the time he had done it for the cash, but also out of a sense of cultivated contempt. Something in him had, for two years, been vehemently denying that night when Silky had come back to him under the lightning-blasted apple tree. He did not believe in ghosts at fifteen.

He had reclined on the straw and the reeds in the barn, now and then drinking from the wineskin the men had provided, vaguely lit by a hanging lamp—the bargain had not stipulated a vigil in the dark. Just before the sun went, his hosts had shown him the place where the ghost came through out of nowhere. They had also shown Parl the cindery glove, pinned to a post in the floor. They had discovered the rudiments, and pointed to the glove, saying, "That's why it comes." Another told how a man had once tried to destroy the glove by throwing it in a hearth fire. But as soon as the thumb began to singe, the man had felt deathly ill. He snatched the glove from the flames before he knew what he was doing. Now they boasted about the deadalive revenant in the barn. They invited travelers to sleep there. The last man who had accepted the bet, they assured Parl, had gone stark mad. Parl had nodded, smiling. He expected tricks but nothing unworldly. He lay on the straw and thought about the bag of silver, which he had convinced himself he wanted. He ignored the sense of horror that lay over the barn. At midnight the ghost came.

It no longer much resembled anything human, though naturally by now it appeared solid and three-dimensional. The physical trauma of its death had stayed with it, which was unusual, and in this case, obscene, for it had been hacked to pieces by enemies. It came from thin air, shrieking with agony, its flesh in ribbons, its eyes put out.

Parl's impulse was normal, and was to run away. Something would not let him. He found himself staggering to the post where the glove was pinned. And the awful, shrieking, eyeless thing came blundering after him. A moment before it

collided with him, Parl cast the wineskin he discovered he
was still holding straight up into the hanging lamp.

The lamp burst with a crack of glass, and fiery oil and
wine splashed over the straw. In seconds, the barn was on
fire, full of light and smoke and roaring. The live dead thing
had by then seized Parl, screaming and pressing him into the
terrible still-bleeding gaping of its wounds. Parl would have
burned along with the linking glove, if somehow the extraordinary power of will that was in him—latent, yet stronger
than any power he had known he had, stronger than muscle
or brain or the drives of hunger, sex, ambition or fear—if
somehow that power had not sprung from him and thrust the
deadalive whining and snarling aside.

The glove flared a few instants later, and the dreadful
noises stopped. The blinded rigid face of the ghost-thing suddenly relaxed, as if its searing hurt had gone away. It faded
quietly in the smoke, and Parl Dro broke out of the barn and
ran like a dog-fox for the wood.

He looked back when he was on higher ground, and saw
the men out in a black silhouette dance around the fire, trying to quench it. He never got their silver, only the name of
an arsonist, and the assured knowledge once more that the
dead did not always die.

The smaller fire between the stones was sinking. Dro
leaned to put on more branches, and paused. Along the side
of the ravine, the musician was playing his music.

Dro sat, the branches loose in his hand, listening. Fine as
silk threads drawn through the dark, the notes sewed over
and about each other. The melody was oblique, tragic, stabbing somewhere inside the heart with a sweet piercing pain,
removed yet immediate. Like that of any excellent minstrel,
Myal Lemyal's music could find out emotions that did not be-
long in the humors or mind of the listener, and plant them
there and let them grow while the song sang itself. But Myal
was much better than excellent. Myal, playing the bizarre instrument his father had killed to get, was one of the lost
golden gods returned from the morning of the earth.

Then a cold sighing came over the ravine, and stars scattered along Parl Dro's spine.

Very slowly, he turned his head, looking beyond the firelight and the freckling leaves of the poplars.

Under the oak on the hill the far side of the gully, glowing a little, like a fungus, shadow-eyed, smiling, still as a stone, sat Ciddey Soban.

Dro got to his feet. She was looking exactly at him, and now, mostly unmoving, she merely followed him with a serpentine turning of her head. She was scarcely transparent any more. Only one limb of the tree showed faintly through the drift of her skirt. Her skin, her hair, were quite opaque. Unlike her sister, this one was strong.

He walked, not fast, along the ravine side, toward Myal's music.

Presently he came to a boulder and saw Myal Lemyal lying against it, sound asleep, and playing the instrument in his sleep.

Dro kicked him in the side. Myal grunted softly, his hands falling over each other and back to the strings, playing on. Dro leaned and slapped him hard across the jaw. The music sheered off, and Myal threw himself into a sitting position, plainly terrified.

"I haven't done anything," he cried, barely awake, the automatic protest of a hundred wrongful, and rightful, apprehensions and beatings.

"Look across the ravine. Then tell me you haven't done anything."

Myal started to look, and then would not.

"What is it?"

"You asked me that on the previous occasion. The answer is the same as then."

"I don't believe you," said Myal, refusing to look.

Dro leaned down to him again, quiet and very dangerous.

"Whether you believe it or not, she's used you. You summoned her with the song. I take it it's a song you composed for her. Now, tell me what else you stole from her corpse."

"Nothing!"

"You insist I search you?"

Myal slithered away backwards along the ground.

"Leave me alone. I tell you, I didn't bring anything, just her shoe—and you burned that."

"You didn't remember the shoe at first. *Think.*"

"I *am* thinking. There isn't anything."

"There has to be something. She's there. She needs a link to *be* there."

"Well, I haven't got anything."

"Back away any farther," said Dro, "and you'll fall down the ravine."

Myal halted himself. He was about a foot from the brink. He hauled himself farther in and, warily watching Dro, stood up.

"I still know I haven't got anything else of hers."

"Then you picked something up without knowing it."

Myal looked as though he might glance across the ravine, but he switched his back to it again.

"Why did she wait till dark?"

"They need the darkness. It's the only canvas they can draw their liars' pictures on. Daylight is for truth."

"I've heard of ghosts being seen by daylight." Dro ignored this. Ridiculously, inappropriately, with death just across the ravine, Myal insisted, "Well, I *have*."

"It's dark now," Dro said, "and she's there."

"Is she really?"

"Look for yourself."

"No, I'll take your word for it. I'm scared. I didn't bring anything but the shoe. I haven't—"

"We'll argue it out later." Dro shifted as if searching for a firmer place to stand. "Tell me, are you right- or left-handed?"

"Both," said Myal. "To play that thing, you have to be."

"She," said Dro, "was left-handed, what I recall of her, as any witch is inclined to train herself to be. That song you played her, have you got it straight in your head?"

"You don't want me to play it? You said—"

"I want you to play it. Backwards."

"What?"

"You heard. Can you do it?"

"No," Myal raised the instrument and studied it. "Maybe."

"Try."

"What happens if I succeed?"

"You get a prize. Her kind are more superstitious even than the living. Reflection, inversion of any sort, might get a response. If it works, she'll go away. Start."

Myal coughed nervously. He settled the instrument. Dro stared across the ravine.

Abruptly Myal began to play furiously, the notes skittering off his fingers. Reversed, the melody was no longer poignant, but of a hideous and macabre jollity, a dance in hell.

Myal, even over the sound of the strings, heard the sudden

female laugh, high and clear as a bell. The noise almost froze
his hands. The hair felt as if it rose on his head at a totally
vertical and ridiculous angle. He shuddered.

"All right," Dro said, "stop now."

"Did it—Is she?—"

"Yes. She's gone."

For the first time, Myal cast a frantic glance across the ravine into the steeping of empty shadows.

Even he could not hide from himself that it had been too
easy. Far, far too easy.

"Last night," said Myal, "I didn't see her then."

"No," Dro said. He began to walk back along the ravine
side toward the low throbbing on the poplar trunks that was
the fire. Myal hung about, terrified of being left alone, but
not attempting to follow. After a moment, Dro looked
around at him. "We'll be traveling together after all," he said.
"I need to keep on eye on you. In case you remember what it
is you did to give her this power through you. The music
helps. But it's more than the music."

Myal held his ground. Angrily he said, "I told you I didn't
see her yesterday. It's nothing to do with me."

Dro said, in that curious voice of his which carried so
softly and so perfectly across the atmosphere of night, "What
did you say to her when she was alive?"

Myal's thoughts poured over. The words stuck up sharp as
flints. He wished they did not. He did not say them aloud.

"If you want my advice . . . you'd run for it."

And she, "Where would I go?"

And he, "Maybe—with me."

He did not say them aloud, but Dro seemed to read them
off his guilty flinching face.

"You'd better understand," said Dro, "you didn't see her
last night, because you weren't near me."

"I don't get it," said Myal. But he did.

And, "Think about it," Dro said. "You will."

Somehow Myal had given Ciddey a path back into the
world, and she utilized him for that purpose. Myal was the
means of her manifestation. But Dro, whom she hated, with
whom she had a score to settle, Dro was the *reason* for her
return. Now, while she had little strength, she might only
trouble them. But when she grew stronger, when Myal, and
her returning phases themselves, had fed her sufficiently—

Dro reached the fire and began to put fresh wood on it. Myal went after him, uneasily skirting each dark thicket and shrub, looking often at the oak tree on the hill.

But in the firelight, Myal relaxed somewhat. Dro had taken up again his position as watchman, though seated, his shoulders resting on a trunk.

Myal sat on the grass, glad to be near the fire. Dro's carven, seemingly immovable figure was a shield between Myal and the night.

"How long are you going to watch?"

"Don't worry about that. Worry about remembering what you may have inadvertently picked up, whatever it is she's using to come through. Rack your brains. It shouldn't be hard with such a limited number."

Myal did not react to that. He was disorientated, so relieved to be no longer alone, he was almost happy. Eventually he asked, in a contrite voice, very aware of its inappropriate request: "You don't have anything to eat, do you?"

Myal emerged from a thicket, flicking burrs off his sleeves with pedantic elegance—the cover for embarrassment—lacing his shirt and hopping, half in his boots, half out.

"I stripped and turned my clothes over."

Dro stood and looked at him.

"I didn't find anything that could have come from *her*. Nothing. Not even a hair."

"All right," Dro turned away.

"Of course, you don't believe me."

"I believe you."

Brashly, Myal said, "Maybe she gave *you* something."

"All she gave me was a claw mark down the side of my face. Which has healed."

"Yes. Heal quickly, don't you? Anything you can't do?"

They ate the portion of bread that was left and drank water from the spring. Myal felt a constant urge to apologize, and started to whistle to prevent himself. Then he became conscious he was whistling Ciddey's song, and went cold to his groin.

Dro started off with no apparent preparation, just rising and walking away. Myal uneasily followed, keeping to the rear, subservient, dog-like and self-hating.

They moved along the side of the ravine, which narrowed and finally closed together. They picked a way down into a valley, and through the valley, and into another valley.

The land had all the same smooth blankness. No smoke rose, there was no stone that had not fallen naturally upon another. There was not even a field which had gone to seed. Not even a ruin. If anyone had ever passed that way he had not lingered, and all trace had been obliterated.

Myal grew jumpy with uneasiness. All his roaming had been at the periphery of towns, villages, courts. He was so ill-prepared for anything like this. He did not even have a bottle to collect drink from springs or streams, having lost the one he had had in an unsuccessful fight half a year before. That he had never thought to replace it was indicative of its unessential quality. Yet, he had gone searching for Ghyste Mortua. For Tulotef.

Where had he first heard of it? Where had the notion of a song of the undead first caught his fancy? He could not recall.

Now, in any case, he had no choice.

And having dogged Dro, begging to accompany him, once Dro was determined that he should, Myal longed to run away. Though run where, and with what ghastly ghostly thing in pursuit?

A wide escarpment floated up from the valley, long dusty concaves of parched and whitened grass, periodically steepled with dark green trees. Near the top, biscuit-colored slashes and streaks of clay daunted Myal with their elevation. Yesterday's ride had knotted the muscles of his legs. At first he had walked the stiffness out. Gradually, it was returning.

Some early currants were beaded along a wild fruiting hedge. Myal tore them off and ate them ravenously. Then he gathered others and advanced on Dro, catching him up for the first time, and offering the gift ingratiatingly.

Rather to Myal's surprise, Dro accepted the currants and ate them, as if he had not noticed them himself.

"It's past noon. When do we rest?" wondered Myal.

"Come now," said Dro, very nearly playfully, "you're not bored with this lovely bracing walk we're having?"

"It beats me why you don't ride with that—with your—well, it beats me. You could afford a horse."

"If I started riding, I'd cease being able to walk anywhere

again," said Dro. "The only way I can keep the damn thing from seizing up forever is to work the hell out of it most days."

"Oh." Awarded this personal revelation, Myal felt pleased and almost flattered. Emboldened, he said, "You seem to know the direct route to Tulotef."

"I practically do. But leave the name alone. Why do you think it got a nickname instead?"

"That other thing," said Myal, "the girl—"

"No," Parl Dro said. "Leave that alone, too."

Puzzled and insecure, Myal did as he was told.

The escarpment went on, up and up. Looking back, the descending lands they had negotiated earlier had become another country, ethereal and far away, perhaps impossible to regain.

Myal's mother had died six months after his birth. Another mistake, getting himself born to a woman who died, probably because of him. Inadvertent matricide thereby added to his crimes. He had been brought up, or dragged up, by the bestial father. At twelve he had run away. He was still running. Still thieving too; his first proper theft had been the stringed instrument—the second time it had been stolen. Before that he had only attempted small robberies, at his strap-wielding father's suggestion.

When the sun fell, and the light began to go, and they were still climbing the inward-curving upland they had first got on to an hour before noon, the analogy of life itself as a hopeless climb occurred to Myal. Though they had rested somewhere, under trees, for a while, his back and his legs screamed. He could not understand how Dro, the cripple, kept going with such seeming indifference, with such a peculiar lurching grace. Myal began to think Dro forced himself on merely in order to spite his companion.

If I stop dead, what then?

Myal stopped dead. Dro did not appear to note the cessation. He went on, walking up into the forerunning brushwork of the dusk.

"Hey!" Myal yelled. "Hey!"

A bird shot out of a tree. Dro stopped, but did not turn. Myal shouted up at him, "I'm not going any farther. It's getting dark."

Then he realized Dro had not stopped because of any of his shouts.

Absurdly, ordered to leave the subject alone, Myal had almost succeeded in wiping it from his mind. A feeling of apprehension which came with the fading of day could be interpreted simply as normal antipathy to another night on hard ground, with possibilities of foraging bears and no supper. Ciddey Soban had been pushed into a corner of Myal's consciousness. He had not wanted to dwell on her.

But now he recollected, and with good reason.

Dro was in front of him, about fifty feet away. Perhaps forty feet ahead of Dro a girl was stepping nimbly up the slope. She did not turn, or hesitate, or threaten, or mock. She was only there, walking, pale as a new star. Ciddey. Terrible, unshakable Ciddey.

Myal swallowed his heart as a matter of course. He went after Dro, prowling, delicate, as if traveling across thin ice. If the girl-ghost turned, he was ready to freeze, change into a tree, dive down a hole—

She did not turn.

He reached Dro. Through the closing curtains of darkness Myal peered at the ghost-killer's impassive face.

"It's not my fault," Myal whispered.

Dro did not whisper, though he spoke softly.

"Maybe. She shouldn't be able to manifest without a link. There doesn't appear to be one. But she's there."

"Do you want me to play the song upside down again?"

"No. I don't think there's much point. I'd say she only left last time out of a kind of scornful sense of etiquette."

"What do we do?"

"Follow her. That's her intention. We might learn something by falling in with it."

"Where's—where's she going?"

"Where do you think?"

"Tulo—the Ghyste."

"The Ghyste. She'd know the road. That's not illogical."

"In every story I ever heard," said Myal, "a vengeful spirit pursues, it doesn't *lead*. Suppose she stops?"

"Shut up," Dro said, still softly. "Start walking."

Myal, forgetting the burning ache in his muscles, walked. They both walked, and Ciddey Soban, not turning, walked before them, into the black cavern of night.

And then the black cavern of night parted seamlessly to let her through, and she was gone.

At first they waited, glancing about for her. Trees grouped together on the slope ahead, hiding what lay beyond. After an unspeaking minute, they went on and through the trees. Nothing stirred, the dark was empty once more. At the edge of the trees, the ground leveled and brimmed over into a great velvet moonless void, like the end of the world, but which was most probably woods.

They looked down at it.

"She's gone," announced Myal. He thought of something. "If she used me to come through, I didn't feel it this time, or last. Only that time in the priests' hostel, when I was sick."

"You're getting accustomed to giving her energy, that's why. That's when it becomes most dangerous."

"Thanks. I feel so much happier now."

Myal sat on the turf, put his arms across his knees and his head on his arms. Despite his words, he was exhausted, and dully afraid.

"We'll see the night out here," said Dro.

"What stupendous fun."

"I mean to wach for three hours. Then it's your turn."

"I'm not watching. I might see something and scare myself to death."

"If you see anything, you wake me. You're watching."

"All right. I'm watching."

An hour later, the moon came up in a long stream of cloud.

Myal was twitchily asleep. Dro stared across the land, keeping quite incredibly motionless, seldom blinking, as if it were his curse, as with certain guardians in myth, to watch forever.

CHAPTER EIGHT

"Oh, Myal," said a girl, licking his ear tenderly. "Oh, Myalmyalmyal."

Myal woke up, already excited and apprehensive.

"Someone call?"

"Oh, Myal," said the girl. "Ohmyal."

She lay on her elbow at his side. Her ash-blonde hair fell across both their faces. He knew who it was, and wondered why he was not petrified. Then it came to him. The simple, obvious solution. Dro had been mistaken, and so had Myal himself. Ciddey was not dead.

When he had dragged her out of the water, he had saved her, just as he desperately meant to do. That she had not revived at once was not utterly surprising. He had been wrong about the strangulated face—a trick of light, and his alarm, the impending fever. No, Ciddey lived, and she had somehow caught them up. She was playing with Dro, punishing him. But she had decided to reveal the truth to Myal, who had rescued her.

"You're not dead," he murmured, vocalizing his thoughts.

"You say the nicest things." She kissed his cheek lightly.

He shivered, with pleasure and nervousness. And then it

occurred to him to look about for Parl Dro. Presently he located a dark inconclusive shape, stretched across the base of
a tree, which had to be Dro. So much for watching. Or . . .
had it been Myal's watch, and had Myal fallen asleep?

"I want you to come with me," said Ciddey Soban,
touching him once more with her real live icy lips.

"Well, I really ought—"

"Don't argue. You know you like me. Let's go for a walk
together. Wouldn't you like that? Down into the wood. It isn't
far."

"Well, all right."

He had gone walking in a wood with the Gray Duke's
daughter. The walk had ended in a pile of leaves, and ultimately, a few months later, in an escape by night, with thirty
of the Duke's men, drunken and murderous and equipped
with mastiffs, in headlong pursuit. Somehow, Myal had got
away. Somehow, he always did. Maybe he was not so
unlucky as he generally believed himself.

With feigned debonair nonchalance, he let the girl draw
him, by her small cold hand, down the slope. Almost inadvertently, he had slung on the instrument as he came to his feet.
Now, as they picked their way among roots and channels in
the earth, the weight of the wood unbalanced him, and he
and she would bump into each other, which was not necessarily displeasing. Minute by minute, Myal grew more excited
and more apprehensive. By the time they entered the first
arching avenues of the woods that walled the end of the
slope, he was feverish and stupidly laughing, clinging to the
girl whenever he could, his heart noisy in his ears, an awful
leaden murmur of warning droning, ignored, in the pit of his
brain.

She, too, undrowned Ciddey, seemed a little fevered. In the
soft, faintly luminescent cave of the wood, she turned and
embraced him. The long, long kiss was cold and marvelous.
Their bodies melted into one another and clamored never to
draw away. In the act of sex, they might literally be turned
into a quivering, gasping, ever-orgasmic tree.

But then she broke away, teasing him. She laughed, and
ran off along the aisle of living columns. He ran after her,
naturally. The shadows of trunks striped over her paleness, so
she seemed to flare on and off like a windblown lamp. Then
suddenly she disappeared.

He had forgotten the supernormal aspect of her former visitations, and dashed toward the spot where she had been, calling her name, partly in anger, and partly because he knew she had meant him to. She would make him desperate, flaunt, tease, elude. When he had reached a stage of sufficient confusion and actual physical discomfort, she would give in.

In a moment, he found her. She had elaborated upon the process of teasing and eluding and flaunting to a unique degree.

A pool lay amid the trees, black and shiny as a slice of highly polished night sky fallen down there. Glancing up, sure enough there was half a white hole in heaven where the piece of sky had come away.

The moon burned on Ciddey at the pool's center, standing in the water, which coiled passively about her knees. She seemed to have grown from the pool, a slender stem, with a flower of face. Her hair was wet, darkened by water at its ends, but she peeled it from her and draped it behind her shoulders. Her dress was all wet and had grown thin and transparent as paper, so he saw her nakedness through it, smokily, unmistakably. Her lips were parted, and smiling, and her eyes heavy. She beckoned to him, urgent as the urgency that now was stabbing through him. Even so, he hesitated, eager to get to her, but not liking the sheen of the water, so cold, so oddly still though she rose from it, smoothing her hair, stirring her limbs a little, beckoning.

"In there?" he asked, hoarse and stupid.

"Yes, oh, yes," she moaned.

At her voice a pang went through him so great that he could no longer bear to keep away. He splashed into the water, clenching his teeth and fists at the cold of it. He thought, in an ecstasy of frustration, she might start to move away from him again as he got closer, but instead she strained her arms to him, though not moving her feet, as if she could not, as if they had grown into the sucking mud on the pool's floor.

He reached her abruptly, and grabbed her. The instrument thumped him on the back. Congratulations. As her snake-like arms curled around him, he knew a moment's horror of the inevitable aftermath, the entanglement, the trap, the complications, but the horror could not keep pace with the anguish of pleasure. The second horror—the possibility of disappointing, failing—had yet to come. It might ruin the supreme moments, or everything might be well, but as yet he did not care. Even the dreary nervous consideration as to how they would manage, nowhere to lie or lean, only the mud and the water underfoot, had not yet taken hold.

Groaning, he submerged, arms, eyes, flesh, mind, full of the girl. All his sight was paleness and darkness, and he could only smell fragrant skin and hair. Her pressure against him was unendurable and he would die without it, and his hands made magic, passing over her, and hers magic in his hair, along his sides, locking him with a fierce strength into the single position he wished to obtain, retain, remain in, cry out in, perish in—

The water exploded.

Thunder caught him by the hair, the shoulder. He was dragged backward. Where he had adhered to her, his body seemed to tear like rent cloth. He yelled insanely, hearing himself. He flailed with his empty arms, sprawled, went down. Water sprang over his head; he gulped it, trying to drink his way back to the air. Something pulled him from the water, turned him. A savage clout across the head rocked him. He half fell again into another hard resilient mass, which in turn dragged him once more.

Crowing for breath, blinded, crazy, he landed on his knees on iron-like earth. He hung his head and coughed water. And the instrument also coughed water from its sound box. As his eyes cleared, he beheld four slender horse legs, shod in metal, pecking at the soil in front of him. And behind those, another four, and another four.

Delight had turned to a dull physical ache. He felt sick. He was afraid. Gradually, he heard the silence of the girl in the pool, and half turning, he glimpsed her. Her face was raw with rage and terror.

Out of his own terror, Myal made himself look up, beyond the legs of the horses.

They wore mail, the three men, and great cloaks, furled like wings. A murky jewel flashed on a hand or wrist. Another smoldered muddy red. Unfriendly faces made of marble and framed by unfriendly courtly wavelets of hair glared at Myal, then at the pool, the girl.

"You," one of the men said, not looking at Myal.

"Me?" asked Myal.

"You are a fool, to go with *that*. Don't you know live flesh from necrophilia?"

Myal choked. He crawled into a bush and attempted to throw up. None of them interfered with him. He heard a dim ominous exchange over his dry spasms. The three riders, some duke's bodyguard or earl's men from the look of them, were haranguing the girl in the pool. They called her filthy names, the word "deadalive" was mingled contemptuously among them. They did not fear her, so much was obvious. They spat on the ground, saying she was a thief. They promised her weird punishments that had to do with graves, worms, flames, wheels. And she, she shrieked back at them, her voice high as a bat's.

Myal slumped on his side, the instrument wedged under his shoulder blade, his knees under his chin. He had some vague incentive to crawl away, to get out of the wood and up the slope, to Parl Dro. Before he could realize the ambition, one of the riders came over, leaned from the saddle, and yanked Myal back again onto open turf. The rider glared at Ciddey.

"There are punishments for those who consort with stray ghosts. The forest hereabouts is rife with bloody undead. Didn't you know? Those who harbor them or encourage the deadalive, deserve to join them. Not gently, either. Like to know some penalties?"

"No, thank you," said Myal politely.

"I'll tell you anyway. There's one school of thought which advocates slashing off the offending part—a hand, say, if you gave them a hand to hold; an ear, if you listened to them, and a tongue if you spoke to them. In your case, rather a nasty amputation, in view of what you were considering doing."

It was so vile, it had to be a joke.

Myal laughed queasily. The men laughed, loud and long, riding around and around him, making his head spin. Then one spurred his horse straight into the pool. The animal looked fearsome as it leaped, eyes rolling, mane flying, the ivory counters of its teeth bared. As the forehoofs hit the water, the rider's hand whirled up, gripping a cleaver of sword. Myal saw Ciddey's white face flung back and the sword crashing down on it. He imagined the impact of skin and bone, green-cinder eyes, kissing mouth, with honed excruciating steel. Someone threw a colorless bag over his head and her scream became a long thin whistle, or a long thin wire, and ceased to matter.

He came to, lying face down in a horse's mane, legs either side in an uncomfortable riding posture, hands securely tied under the beast's neck.

The horse was running. Two other horses ran, one on each side. The right-hand horse had two riders, the left seemed strangely overcrowded too, but its nearer rider held the reins of Myal's horse firmly in his fist.

Everything had ended, inevitably, in misery, mistake and injustice.

Surely when they killed the girl, they had become aware she was not a ghost? Maybe that made them more dangerous. Was it her corpse over the second horse? Supposedly, any who lived at all close to such a legend as the Ghyste, would be unreasonably wary of apparitions. Myal should have thought of that, so should Ciddey.

Ciddey. . . .

The idea of her filled him with fright. Not because of her death by the sword, suddenly, but because—because— *Could it be these madmen had been correct?* Perhaps the sword was holy in some way and could effect exorcism—Myal had heard, even sung, of such things. If she had been dead. . . . He felt himself on the verge of passing out again, and struggled to keep hold of reality.

"Where are we going?" he asked the men, those courtly riders. The question was familiar. He had asked Dro, the morning he had had the fever, also slung over a horse, the same thing. Dro had not answered. One of the men did, in his fashion.

"It's a surprise. Excited?"

The horse bounced over a gap in the ground. Myal slid, the instrument slammed him in the spine and the animal's withers slammed him in the face.

He cursed the instrument with hysterical relief that it was still with him.

Everything else was horrifying and Myal was helpless. He might as well pass out again, there was nothing he could do. The colorless bag swung up once more and he rolled over into it.

"No," someone said.

Myal's head was wrenched around. A black fiery juice trickled into his mouth. He swallowed, gagged, swallowed. The horses were static. There was an undeniable sense of arrival. Somewhere.

Myal opened his eyes.

He could not see very far, or very much, from his sideways face-down position, but they seemed to be on some kind of bridge or causeway. Beyond lay open night, towers and turrets of forest shearing away. Forward, there was light.

One of the men bent over Myal, obscuring the limited view completely.

"No, you mustn't faint any more."

"Sorry," muttered Myal.

"We want you to ride in proudly. There's no pride for us having caught you if you snivel and swoon and sprawl all over the horse like a bundle of washing."

"No, I can see that."

"If you're good, we'll let you sit upright."

"And when we get through the gate, you could shout and thrash about a bit," said another, smoothly. "The notion being that you're brave, and furious at capture. Do you see?"

"Then we'll cuff you, beat you into submission. It'll look fine. So will you."

"I'd rather—" said Myal. A voice cut him short.

"I've a better idea," said the voice.

He could not twist his head any farther, could not see. Then he no longer needed to.

"Well," said the bending man, "what's your idea, Ciddey?"

"My idea," said the voice of Ciddey, "is that I rope him about the neck with a ribbon, and lead him in that way. You can follow."

The men laughed. The laugh was dark and menacing.

"You're bold, for a newcomer," said one.

Ciddey did not laugh. She slipped from the second horse. She walked to where Myal lay, his head turned painfully to stare at her.

"What a pity, though," she said, "I don't seem to have a ribbon."

Suddenly the bonds that held Myal to the horse's neck

gave way, untied or cut by one of the men. Myal lay, with his arms dangling, till one of the others pulled him upright.

"Are you bewildered, Myal Lemyal?" asked Ciddey Soban. She put her hand on his thigh. Her hand was cold as winter snow. "They didn't kill me. It was a test. They do kill. But not—a friend."

Then Myal looked ahead.

He saw the sloping crenellated walls, the sturdy gates, the light of lamps that overpowered the light of the stars and phantomized the moon. And far below, he made out the inner rim of a colossal water. Though from this vantage he could see only two of its starlike raying channels.

One of the men slapped him on the arm, a hard freezing slap. Myal knew it all by then. He did not need them to say to him, one by one, most courteously, "Welcome to Tulotef."

After an interval of oblivion, Parl Dro opened his eyes.

He had told Myal to wake him after three hours, but Dro had not reckoned Myal would last so long. Dro's inner clock had roused him accordingly.

He woke silently and stilly, fully alert within seconds. Not yet moving, he let his eyes seek over the ridge. He had registered immediately that the musician was absent, but that the instrument remained, propped by a tree, trailing its sling like a frayed embroidered tail. Dro might have assumed Myal had stolen off for the usual private purpose of nature, save that, to Dro, the whole area seemed imperceptibly to sing and glow, as if some kind of mineral had fallen from the sky.

Presently Dro sat up, rose, walked across to the spot beside the instrument where Myal had been sitting. The grass was still flattened somewhat—not by a seated figure, but a prone one. Myal had slept at his watch as Dro had grimly predicted. Looking at it, Dro felt the familiar signals, the shift of hair on scalp and neck, the tiny ratlike beast which seemed to scuttle up his spine.

Parl Dro stood and looked toward the sea of forest that flooded the valleys below. The moon was high, but there was scarcely any wind to bring the muted sounds of the woodland up to the ridge.

Then he heard the thin clear note, like that of a bird, or even of a reed pipe, piercing acutely as a needle through the shadow and the foliage a mile below.

There was nothing else, or nothing else he heard.

The fire was almost dead. Dro killed it quickly and thoroughly with a couple of blows.

He picked up Myal's musical instrument, held it a moment, then, unwillingly, slung it across his own shoulders. Its touch, weight, shape and aura—of another man's inner world?—disturbed him.

Abruptly, Dro spoke one foul obscenity to the night. Then he swung himself off the ridge and onto the tricky ground that led almost vertically into the forest. Presently, in the bushes a couple of feet down the slope, he kicked against something, glanced at it, and found Myal Lemyal's body.

He was lame, and now he carried the dead weight of a nightmarish hell-harp on one shoulder, the dead weight of a man over the other. The man, it was true, was thin and therefore light to carry. Even so, it was nothing he would have wished on himself.

Random, primitive tracks scattered through the forest, as if several balls of twine had been dropped, allowed to roll at will and then metamorphosed into pathways. The night had added a second forest to the first, having planted quick seedlings there at dusk, which rapidly shot up into tall, thick-boled trees made entirely of shadow, and which blocked every aisle and avenue.

Dro had gone by a dry watercourse, a chasm of moss and undergrowth where once there had shimmered a pool. The place shimmered still, a psychic shimmer. The cry Dro had heard on the ridge had come from this spot.

He began to follow a purely unphysical path, then. A kind of razor-edged blind brilliance only he could see.

The moon swung over and away behind him, barely noticed through the gloom and the foliage. Once a fox ran across the invisible track, narrowing its eyes, bristling with fear at the vibrations of the deadalive, which painted the tips of the grasses like fire.

Then, at last, the day began to come.

With sick relief, and with anger, Parl Dro felt the clue fading out on the ground, the air.

Ahead, the night trees planted between the real ones began to crumble and dissolve. Pink dawn sprang through instead.

The world opened out into great new spaces; a blade carved the wood, and everything of night was gone, including the vile and shrilling road to Ghyste Mortua the dead had left behind them.

Dro cursed, the same curse as before. He eased the musician's body off his back, and let it fall haphazardly, the musical instrument in its wake. Dro sat on a fallen tree, and slowly stretched out before him the biting, howling, shrieking torturer which his lame leg had become.

He sat and watched the forest as it flushed and brightened. Birds dived in and out of pools of light. But his agony was so huge it had temporarily deafened him, and he had not, nor could not, hear their voices.

Neither did he hear the crackling sound the sled made. Or rather, he heard it, but did not spontaneously react. When he finally convinced himself that someone was near, and he should care about the fact, he turned and found the woman standing ten feet away, the rough-made sled, loaded with branches, attached to her hands by two fraying corded ropes. The young sun hit her squarely, and she, by contrast, looked old as the hills. But, black-mantled and black-eyed, she might have been some ancient sister of his.

"Nice day," she said, in a voice like a rusty bolt.

"Uh."

She dropped the ends of rope and walked over.

"Not for you, though," she said.

She kneeled, rusty as her voice, on the earth before him, reached out and clamped her two withered hands on the blazing shrieking leg. Anyone but Dro would have cried out. She said to him, just as if he had, "Keep faith. You'll see."

He saw. The intolerable agony cut up through guts and ribs into his throat, and went out. A slow cool warmth soaked from the old woman's hands. She twisted and pummeled the muscles of his calf and the bones beneath. Great shocks of pain went off, and the cool warmth flowed in after them. He slumped back on the tree and started to go to sleep, but held himself just over the threshold into waking. After a long wonderful time, her hands went away. She sat on the ground, put off her hood and began to braid thin trails of dark gray hair.

"To thank you is inadequate," he said. "What fee do you usually ask?"

She darted a look at him.

"Three thirty-penny pieces."

He smiled slightly. She was poor. Ninety pence was wealth to her, her face gone greedy and feral thinking of it.

"I don't imagine that's enough."

"It's enough. The cure won't last."

"I know."

He started to get coins out of his clothes to give her. His hands moved lazily and it was difficult to count.

The leaves overhead had eyes of gold in them. He lay and looked back at them. He did not want to move ever again, and so eventually he sat up. The dull, bearable, normal pain woke in his leg. He had known it would. Though it had seemed gone forever, no healer could rid him of that. He reached over and put five thirty-pence pieces in her lap.

"All right," she said. "That'll do." She stared at Myal Lemyal's body sprawling on the grass. "Where were you taking him? Home, for burial?"

Dro recognized her dimly, part of the pattern of things. He had met representations of the virgin and the nubile woman. Here was one of the crone. Maid of Vessels, Queen of Fires, and this one, Queen of Swords. Truly, a sister.

"He isn't," said Dro quietly, "dead."

"He looks it. No breathing. No drum sound in the chest."

"His heart beats. Once every few minutes."

"Well I never," said the crone-queen. She got up and went to Myal, bent, creaked, kneeled and stroked his hair. "Is it a trance you're in, baby?" she asked Myal softly. "Poor baby. Hush-a-bye." Then she drew her hand off Myal's hair. "Now," she said. "Now. There's something—"

"Ghyste Mortua," said Dro.

"Yes, yes." She was impatient. "And you are a ghost-killer, and this one a minstrel wanting to make a song of the Ghyste and be famous. Didn't you ever warn him? He'll never be a success, he's too good. Too good a musician to be famous or to be loved. He's a genius. He'll never be recognized in his own time. We only revere the rather good, the very good, not the best, never the best. Not until they're safely dead, and can't take advantage and hurt us. Never applaud a magician. For his next trick he might eat the world. Ah!" she exclaimed. "One heartbeat. Yes, I saw it, in his throat. Help me put him on the sled."

"If I left you money," said Dro, "you might look after him, while I get on."

"Aren't you curious," said the crone, "about the cause of the trance?"

"The deadalive have been feeding off him."

"It's more than that. Help me put him on the sled."

Dro went by her, lifted Myal and laid him on his back on the sled, on top of the piled branches, which snapped and broke. Dro took up the instrument, and next the corded ropes. His leg complained, sour, easy to ignore.

"Which way?"

The old woman nodded. She waddled ahead of him, going south between the trees.

Ten minutes later, he followed her into a clearing. The eyelets of sun fell on the ground and splashed the walls of a stone hovel. It had been in existence some decades, and the foundations had considerably subsided into the earth. Bright herbs or weeds flowered in a patch near the leaning door. A wooden post stood up there, with two hands made of weather-stained plaster clasping each other on top, probably the local sigil for a healer. Daubed eccentrically on the leaning door, difficult for him to decipher, were the words: SABLE'S HOUSE.

Dro wondered briefly who came here. Presumably there was a village or a town adjacent, though he had seen no sign of one piercing the forest, from the ridge above. Or maybe the town had been abandoned, encroached on by the trees, by poor living, by famine or a plague. And only the old woman remained, somehow keeping alive, though how was rather a mystery.

She thrust open the door, and motioned Dro to drag the sled and the death-tranced man inside. It was a dark room, still full of the night. It smelled of damp and the low smoky fire, and soon of the two fat-tallow candles she lit in the walls. There was a herbal smell also, and pots, buckets and urns were stacked in all directions. A bundle of rags in the corner was the bed, and here Dro was instructed to set Myal.

Sable—that was, one assumed, her name—came over and peered down at Myal, who looked as dead as any dead man Dro had ever seen, and yet was not.

"Was he skilled at trancing himself?" Sable inquired.

"Not to my knowledge."

"You knew him well?"

"No. But well enough to know that, I think."

"It isn't any ghost brought him to this," said Sable. "It was a live one. Healer. Herbalist. Meet anyone like that, eh?"

"Only one who played with it, and she's dead."

"There's a drug can do this," said Sable. "It turns life down low, like a lamp, just a spark left burning. And with a psychic talent, that lets the spirit out. You know what that means, ghost-killer? It means you have the ghost of a man that's still alive."

"All right. But how did she do it?"

"I'll tell you how. In a minute. Got a knife?"

Dro studied her, then took out the knife and handed it to her, hilt first. The courtesy made her laugh soundlessly. Then she bent and ripped the knife along Myal Lemyal's chest. In the dull light, it took Dro a moment to realize it was the shirt, not the man, she was quartering. With careful delicacy she picked off the leaves of cloth with the knife, not touching them with her fingers. A pocket had been torn and certain obtuse items dropped from it onto Myal's skin: a copper coin with a hole through it, a defaced die, a coil of wire that might have had to do with the musical instrument, a little clay dog.

Dro knew the dog at once, and could not remember from where. First he pictured it tied to the wheel of a wagon. Then he saw Cinnabar in the glint of her oven, pinching the dog from clay.

Sable shifted the dog aside, using the knife. There was a faint transparent mark on Myal's flesh where the dog had rested. The torn cloth of the pocket was damp.

Involuntarily, Dro leaned forward.

"Don't touch," said Sable. "The little animal's clay, and the clay's been made porous. The drug's been poured inside, and then seeped out after a while, right through clay and cloth and skin. Tactile poison. Doesn't need to be drunk, just touched. Carried over the heart, where he carried it, it did very nicely. Gradual, you understand, bit by bit—then whoof! Out like a candle, and the spirit gone away. He must have done something she didn't like. Lady's man, was he?"

"Not exactly. Can you wake him up?"

"Not exactly. I'll move the clay animal and the drug will stop seeping into him. We know he's psychic. If he's strong enough, the spirit can try to get back. Or if he isn't, it won't. In any case, it'll take days. Days and nights."

CHAPTER NINE

The sun moved and increased its fire, and came to stream through the hovel's open door.

Sable brewed herbal tea, which she trickled into a little iron cup and handed to Dro. There seemed to be no food in the hovel, or possibility of food outside. Not even mushrooms, let alone a chicken, a cow, apple trees or vines. Probably she lived on the tea.

As he drank it, a green sweet-sore memory passed through Parl Dro. He identified it reluctantly. Sable's brew was like the tea Silky's grandmother had concocted, in that spick-and-span town hovel almost thirty years in his past.

They did not speak for a long while, keeping as silent and almost as quiet as Myal on the bed of rags. Matter-of-factly, Sable had stripped the musician and worked over his body, massaging with her extraordinary hands. She displayed none of the easily tickled, impotent lust of the elderly, nor much concern. Twice, she asked Dro to turn the younger man's body. Finally, she had him placed on his back, his head slightly averted toward the right shoulder, and a ragged, not unduly filthy sheet, pulled up over him.

The sunlight, creeping like a cat, had almost reached Myal, when Dro spoke to her.

"Tell me about Ghyste Mortua."

She looked at him, and sucked her tea.

"You know all you need to."

"You live on the doorstep," he said. "You'd know more."

"The woods are full of noises by night," she said. "Riders, horses, yellings. They don't bother with me. I'm too old, too near the edge, the gate out. Too ugly. They don't bother."

"Your village," said Dro. "Is the Ghyste what drove your people away?"

"That, and other things. But if you're asking have the deadalive got stronger in these parts, yes, they have. Stronger, and stronger still. I haven't got the seventh sense, but when I was a girl," she said, "I'd see shapes in the wood like milk, pale, showing the trees through them. Now, the dead look like men. I'll tell you, when I spotted you in the dawn, I wondered."

"They're strong enough to manifest after sunrise?"

"They're strong."

"But only at certain seasons," said Dro.

"Of course. What'd you expect? The psychic time that corresponds with the time of the landslide. Not a calendar day or month or year. But moon times, star times, seasons of conjunction and the zodiac. One is right now. That's why you're here, eh? And him—somehow he knew the right time, too. So he's cleverer than you think."

"Or than he thinks."

"Solved your mystery yet?" she inquired. "I mean the woman who made the clay dog, and put the drug into it, and why."

"Maybe."

"What'll you do?"

"What *will* I do?"

"It's easier," said Sable. "Her way, it's easier. Especially for you, Parl Dro."

"So you know my name," he said flatly.

"I guessed your name," she said. "People always said, one day you'd come."

The old pain gnawed sullenly on the bones of his leg. Pain like fear.

And the memory began to come he had been trying to keep at bay. He had shoved the memory out of sight in some attic of the mind. He had thrust other memories in its way, between himself and it. Memories of childhood, of youth. Even of Silky. Rather be wounded than made a fool, perhaps.

But now, he slipped back toward it. The herb tea, the pain, Myal's half death, the message Cinnabar had sent, all these things pushed Dro back along the highway in his brain. Not far. He found himself glancing over five years, then over more than twenty. At himself, fifteen, twenty-five, thirty-five. The years of growing and learning, by trial and error, by thought and reading and dialogue, his inescapable trade. He glimpsed two or three old men, professional exponents of exorcism, those who had taught him. He had never really needed their lessons. Somehow he had known. Always known, and always had the strength, psychic, metaphysical, to put the knowledge to its terrible, essential work. Silky, when he was thirteen, had found the truth of his calling in him, just as, if she had not died, she would have found for him other truths, better, sweeter, less precious. And if she had lived, how would he have lived? A farmhand to this day, perhaps. Or a minor landowner if he was lucky. Sons and daughters, a wife, a gradual, gentle, back-breaking, marvelously simple life. If she had lived, and not come to him in the rain with her cold hands and her elemental wickedness. But he could not linger with Silky. The memory he was avoiding was nearer than that. Very, very near. Not a boy of thirteen, a man dressed in black. And yet, of course, Silky was in this memory, too. Had almost been the cause of it.

He could see the mountain with absolute clarity. It was ahead of him in the memory, poking up in the dusk to the northeast, like a chimney, smoking a single cloud and a scatter of spark-bright early stars. Over the mountain lay the lands that drew away into the legend, the mirage that pulled at him, Tulotef, Ghyste Mortua. He knew the season for it was coming, as every few years it did, the time of manifestation. Philosophers and charlatans had all instructed him, and he had believed in it with a dry matter-of-fact mysticism.

Strange, though, how dim and amorphous that initial belief in the Ghyste seemed to him now, as he recollected it. More a casual interest than a driving goal, not the dedication it had become.

Probably what happened, the trouble before he crossed the mountain, had influenced him. He was contrary enough so that to have obstacles apparently put in his way made him more determined to press on.

The slopes of the south side of the mountain were lightly wooded, the trees folding back to those farther mountains south and west, that had grown so vague in the dusk, as if they were only paintings, which ran.

A clearing dipped through the wood. A bit of the sun had shone from it during the sunset and now burned on a nest of wood. A firelit wagon hulked nearby, with a scrawny, moth-eaten dog tied to the wheel, but no horse in sight. Dro had come on the scene abruptly, and paused. The dog, scenting or hearing him belatedly, set up a racket, trying to offset its aberration by sheer volume. Dro was faintly amused by this, also alert to see some man come around the wagon or between the trees, brandishing axe or knife or staff. Instead, a woman appeared, and empty handed.

She stood and looked at Parl Dro across the forty-foot space between them, and gave him one of the great shocks of his existence. For she was Silky, Silky to the life—or would it be the death? And worse than seeing a mere child again, this was Silky as she might have grown to be, a woman of early middle years, a little coarsened, a little fined, but the scintillant hair still like molten honey in the firelight, spilled over her back, her breasts.

Before he knew it, he had begun to walk toward her, not even really wanting to, but impelled.

The dog dropped its histrionics to a guttural growling, and the woman who was Silky retreated to the wheel, and put her hand out ready to loosen the rope that kept the dog tied.

When Dro came on, she shouted at him.

"Who are you? How dared you sneak up on me? Don't you know my man'll soon be here and see to you?"

Obviously a bluff. The dray horse was gone, and the man with it. That meant a longish journey at best.

"I don't mean you any harm," Dro called.

He breathed more easily since she had shouted, for her voice was not like Silky's voice, even allowing for the intervening years.

Yet her face—the closer he got, the more it seemed to him

that Silky was here. Between one step and the next, he had
the terrifying meditation that maybe a ghost could not only
cheat death, solidify, appear to all the senses to be mortal
flesh, but, into the bargain—the ultimate cheat—could appear
to mature, to age. Why not? If a ghost could survive, blotting
out the nature of its death, swindling itself eventually into
crediting its own "true" life, then surely it must be capable of
supposing itself into growing up and growing old, along with
the rest of living humanity.

But he had destroyed Silky's link. Released her—murdered
her—

The woman was beautiful. Richly beautiful. There was a
heavy abundance to her, despite her lean and fragile build,
that found its utmost expression in the welter of honey hair.
Her skin, summer-tanned, was honey too, the small lines like
cracks over gold leaf. On her hand was a brass ring. There
really was a man somewhere, then. But not here.

Dro slipped off the hood of his cloak. Walking slowly, his
lameness was minimized, and he was graceful. He kept his
hands loose, free of the mantle, showing that he himself had
no weapon ready or considered.

The woman stared hard in his face, then suddenly relaxed.
She took her hand off the dog's rope and looked down at it.

"Hush," she said. "It's all right."

"Thank you," said Dro, "for taking me on trust."

"Only a fool would judge you a robber," she said boldly.
"As for rape, would you ever have to?" She colored at her
own words, but met his eyes as she said it. "Where are you
making for?"

"Over the mountain."

She said, "My man's gone that way. Gone to do business
with another man. Buy something, or steal it, the bastard. He
won't be back till tomorrow. If he comes back then. If he
isn't lying blind drunk in some inn somewhere with some
woman somewhere. If he isn't too drunk to have a woman.
I'm sorry."

The dog had stopped growling and lay down with its sad
muzzle on its thin paws. The woman walked away to the fire
and used a long skewer to pick a meaty bone out of a pot
which sizzled there. The dog rose, salivating pathetically as
the woman waved the bone to cool it. Presently she placed

the bone on the ground before the dog, and as it began to gnaw its meal, she caressed it with a painful tenderness.

"Poor thing," she said to Dro, speaking of the dog as if about a child. "My man beats him, starves him. He'd do better on his own in the woods. He'd turn into a wolf and be happy. I tell him, the dog, I promise him, one night I'll let him go, untie him and send him off. Then *I'll* get the beating. But I will, one night. Won't I, dog?" She glanced at Dro, who had stood there motionless all this while, watching her. "You'll think I'm daft, I expect."

"No."

"You will. But you're welcome to share the stew with me. I can't feed the dog and not offer something to you."

"You could."

"I'd rather you didn't go," she said. "He just left me here, but I'd rather there was a man by. We came up from the south, do you see. This country's new to me." She straightened and looked at him. Her throat was delicate as if carved, the skin stretched taut, yet silken. Through it he could see her heart thudding.

"I'd like to stay, if you want me to," he said.

She smiled, and said, "Yes, but that's not an invitation, mind." By which he knew it was.

He wondered stupidly if he in turn reminded her of some other, or if she were merely a slut, or simply lonely. Women were constantly attracted to him, and to the half-truth about celibacy and psychic power, and whether a ghost-killer would or not. Or did she not guess his calling.

They ate by the fire, and then she brought out a skin of beer, and they drank together. She began to comb her fingers through her hair until it became an electric crackling blizzard of golden smoke. She sang to the flames drowsily, her voice light and throbbing. She was making an intuitive magic, all of it for him. As Silky had done in the apple tree, sun in her hair, murmuring to birds or leaves . . . and when he spoke to her now, she gazed at him, unsurprised as Silky had been.

"Can I pay you for the meal?"

"I don't think so," she said.

They spoke about the season for a while, and about the showman's trade her husband intermittently practiced. She asked Dro nothing, not even his name. He did not ask hers

either. He could not have called her by it, just as he could
never have brought himself to call her "Silky." The whole ep-
isode was dreamlike, transient.

The dog slept on its side, turned also to gold by the firelight, then to ruby as the flames sank low.

When they each leaned to cast a branch on the fire, their
bodies finally touched. The act of sex had become so inevitable and so desired between them that he seemed to have
had her before, many times. Everything was familiar, without
hesitation, awkwardness or apology. She was lovely, even
what the years had softly faded, or etched with their gold,
was lovely, in her.

Afterwards, they lay wrapped together by the fire. The
wood breathed. Their own breathing lulled both of them
asleep, and later woke them again.

About an hour before sunrise, the whining of the dog
roused Parl Dro.

It was cold, the clear wet chill that dripped through the
trees before a summer dawn. The fire was out. The woman,
showered over by her summer hair, lay sleeping on her side.
Her face was cupped into one hand. One bare full breast
gleamed out against her own tawny color, startlingly snow-
white. The dog stood, hackles raised. A horse cropped the
turf nearby. Beside the wagon was a man.

He looked almost every inch the uncouth robber the
woman had feared the night before. From that alone, Dro
recognized him as her husband. Squat, dirty and disheveled,
he poised in a bizarre kind of half crouch, hair and clothes
flopping, and a loose gut flopping before all that. Only the
man's hands were curious, thin and articulate, though
crammed now into raw red fists.

"Well," he said, slurred and drunken and all too lucid,
"well, well, well."

The situation was laughable, the pith of many an inn song
and joke. Dro got to his feet slowly, pulling his clothes together as he did so, and the man winked malevolently,
leering.

"Well, *well*, well."

Dro said nothing, and then the man thought of some more
words.

"Aren't you going to say: It's all a bad mistake? Aren't

you going to say: Just because you found me lying between your wife's legs, I don't actually have to have been doing anything with her? Well?"

"I'll say all that, if you like," Dro said.

"Like? *Like*?" The man straightened. He stepped over a leather sack on the grass—robber's booty? As he passed the dog, not looking at it, it cowered. He came walking through the ashes of the fire. "You forced her," said the man. "Right? She was unwilling and you raped her."

"Yes. I raped her."

"She looks raped. I must say. Definitely raped."

Dro was aware the woman had woken and sat up, but he did not turn to her. The man was now close enough that the stench of ill-digested alcohol on his breath struck Dro's nostrils. Dro moved an inch or so, coming between husband and wife in the only manner left.

"I think," said the man, smiling down at his wife, "she was slightly willing."

Dro moved, his fist already rising, left arm already extending to block any move the other man might make. But the woman was on her feet, catching back Dro's arm.

"No," she panted. "*No*. It's all right."

"Of course it is," said the man. "Why should I care? I've been with a whore all night." He beamed at Dro. "Both been with whores. Yours any good? Mine was."

The woman began to push Dro fiercely.

"Go away. Please. Go away now."

She was breathless. Dro said, "You'd better come with me."

"Who'll cook my breakfast?" asked the man aggrieved. "Come on, I don't care." He sat down by the dead fire and took off his boots carefully. "Let's have some service," he said.

The woman, holding her dress together over her white breasts with her brown hands, took up the beerskin and handed it to her husband.

"Thanks," he said. He drank noisily.

"Go away," the woman said to Dro. "I'm begging you."

"All right. But you—"

"*Go*."

In the deadly still quarter dark Parl Dro started to walk

away. At the clearing's edge, he looked back and she was lighting the fire. The man drank from the skin. The dog lay like a rock, and the horse plodded about the turf.

Dro walked out of sight, and waited. Nothing happened. At last the sun rose. The woman appeared out of the trees when he had given her up. She stood some yards from Dro and cried in a low wild voice: "Didn't I say you must go? If you get off, he'll be all right. He's only a great baby. Go now, like I told you. Damn you, you're nothing to me. He's my *man*."

For a while, Dro walked slowly, listening for her to scream. The wood rustled and chirped with birds. Nothing else. He began to be able to convince himself she had known what she did, and that everything would be well. She had had, after all, a choice. Dro could have protected her. She was not obliged to stay with such a man as the drunkard.

She ceased to resemble Silky. She became a woman he had spent a night with. The circumstances of discovery were embarrassing and futile.

By the time he reached the track that led up from the trees to the mountain, it was noon. He had swallowed the incident down like bitter medicine. And, in the way of solitary unique events, it had become unreal.

He was about half a mile away from the pass, when the woman's man caught up to him.

Dro heard the clatter of hoofs on the slate and stone of the track, knew, and turned around. But the man seemed to burst out of the very air. There had been time to gain an advantage, yet Dro had not tried for one. His contempt for the man, his contempt for the woman who would stay with such a brute, and his contempt for himself, tangled, however briefly, between them, made Dro stand there arrogantly at the wayside, waiting, in full view.

Of course, he was remembering the absence of weapons, the balled, empty weakling's fists. But this time the man had armed himself with a long dull swerve of violence which Dro never properly saw. Because, unspeaking, preplanned, malicious in cunning and in accuracy, the man swung and delivered his blow in the exact moment he came level with Parl Dro. Nor did he aim where he might have been expected to—at head or heart, or even, with an obscene aptness, at the groin. Yet the target of the blow was, nevertheless, both obscene and apt. He hurled the unidentified weapon with all the force of his fermented compost-heap hate, at Dro's crippled left leg.

One second then, Parl Dro was a thinking man, astonished, outmaneuvered in the quiet afternoon. Next second he was a howling mindless thing flung down into a hell that knew neither night nor day, nor any time at all save the hour of his agony.

He understood after, he had fallen over and away, rolling off the side of the track, through stone defiles, gaunt thickets, along the mountain's hollow flanks, in a cascade of shale. He fetched up in a narrow channel with one broken wall, and if he had gone farther it would have been off the mountain entirely, into space and presumably annihilation. In any event, he knew none of that till much later.

He came to once, in a roar of pain. He had been dreaming of the pain, even unconscious, dreaming that the ghost-thing on the bridge was at work on him once more. He seemed soaked in hot water, or sweat. The avenger had not followed him, had been unable to, or unable to discover him. But he had forgotten that, too. The pain was not localized. It was a sea, and he floundered in it, screaming. And then he died again. He went on like that, dying and waking, dying and waking, for a long while, or rather a timeless while. He never positively knew, when at last he began to reason again, how long he had lain in that channel of the mountain.

When eventually he was able to think, he was amazed, for the leg was not even broken—every bone had seemed splintered, and the splinters mashed.

When he got free of the channel, it was night, and the moon was shining. From the shape of the moon, and certain horrible, barely recalled revivals, he deduced he had been lying there two or three days.

The hurt in the leg had subsided to a blaze, as if the muscles and tendons were merely on fire. It was the damaged nerves of the previous wounding, ill equipped to endure another wound, which had so incapacitated him.

His return to consciousness was marked by a frantic feverish compulsion to get to the woman.

He had incoherently realized by then, naturally, that her

pleas that he go away had been entirely for his sake. She had known what "her man" was capable of, and foolishly had put Dro first. If she had instead appealed to him for help, they might both have fared so much better.

Scrambling down from the mountain was difficult. The agony it cost him went almost ignored, save when he fell and lay in the slate dust, the stars darkening with the blood behind his eyes. In the end, the descent grew more facile. He became used to staggering on the blazing stick of leg.

Night, and somehow another day were gone, before he reached the clearing in the wood. The wagon was gone, too. In the dark he could not find the wheel ruts traced over the turf and summer-hard soil. He could not even find the remains of the fire.

He began to search, idiotically, about the wood, wandering in circles mostly. Day and night blended. He came on a deserted farm at the wood's edge. A few roots and other vegetable stuff were coming up wild in the garden patch, and there was a well. It was enough to keep him alive, and gradually to bring him back to logic and fatalism.

He lost track of time again in the farm ruin. Not for many years had he been so indecisive, so plainly lost over the horizons of his own self. The days seemed very hot, the nights interminable. The old house looked out southward from the wood, into the slender valleys that lay between the claws of the southern mountains. Seen mainly by night, they did not seem real either. Indeed, nothing did.

In the end, the idea of the Ghyste came back to him, supplanting other ideas or regrets. To travel across the northern mountain again became imperative—to go after the legend.

The memory of the woman who was like Silky became frankly an embarrassment. Whatever had been done to the crippled leg, it had healed into its usual awful acceptable state. The same could occur with memory.

As he came over the mountain pass, down the steel-blue road in the dusk, toward that leaning macabre house with its stone tower—the house of Ciddey Soban, the house of the ghost—he had a wonderful sharpened sense of returning to reality, and to purpose. The golden woman slipped away from him like a dream.

He could have done nothing for her. Trouble had caged her. He could not have set her free. He had not loved her, certainly. He had never loved, woman or man, place or beast or object. Not even Silky. Silky had only been a part of himself.

CHAPTER TEN

Sable was plaiting her thin iron hair again, as she came into focus for him across the hovel, but the sun no longer shone on the rag bed where Myal Lemyal lay immobile on his back, head still averted toward the right shoulder, the grimy sheet pulled to his adam's apple, unruffled by any movement.

"You've been away a long while," said Sable. "Thinking, or else you sleep with your eyes wide open. I could count the times you blinked on the fingers of one hand. Practicing?"

Dro watched her pointlessly busy, agile and magical paws.

"You mean I'd prefer to use my own will, rather than Cinnabar's drug, to get there? That was always the plan."

"Then don't you wonder why she sent this boy in ahead of you?"

"She thought she saw something in the cards she cast. She told me. She insisted Myal must go with me. She persuaded him after me. He had some supernatural baggage with him I could have done without."

He had grasped Cinnabar's scheme with slight surprise. That she foisted the musician on him by the means of loaning Myal a horse was eccentric enough. The drug in the clay dog, which had subsequently tranced Myal and loosed his astral body, as near equivalent to a ghost as a live man could go, was a ridiculous ploy.

Cinnabar must have learned from her lover, that ghostkiller who never returned, that the ultimate way into Ghyste Mortua had to be in spirit alone. Those who were dragged in live through the manifested ghost gates of Tulotef invariably died, so the story went. That death would be inevitable to a human taken there quick, with so many deadalive feeding their unflesh hungrily on his life force—even if they did not actually lay their claws on his skin and bones. So, only by releasing astral from physical could a man get in that place and hope to survive. By becoming as near a ghost as the ghosts of the Ghyste. To this end, there were disciplines to be learned, and Dro, who also knew the story, had accordingly learned them, a smattering here, a smattering there, all knotted together by his will. That will of pure iron, which carried him mile after mile, striding on a raging ruin called, euphemistically, a leg. That same iron will, he had believed, could put to sleep Dro's body's life and let the spirit out. Could hold the body intact in its trance, and, if any were able to achieve it, could bring the spirit back into the body, when he was done with Tulotef.

But Myal. Flung out in spirit like a handful of dust on the air. Caught by the deadalive, no doubt of that, and by the virgin, the Maid of Vessels, with her fish-cool hate and her illusory streams—Cinnabar had consigned Myal to that, because she had been sure his proximity was in some form vitally necessary to Parl Dro. If Dro must enter Tulotef, then Myal must be there before him. It would have been good to judge Cinnabar as mad, to be irritated by her conviction and methods. But, with unease, Dro had recognized in her one of those mysterious guides the psychic road was liable to produce. And she had reminded him of the golden woman in the wood. Queen of Fires, Queen of Leaves—

The Queen of Swords, his eldritch elderly sister, was brewing more tea. The aromatic steam curled across the hovel, and vanished as if passing through the walls: the ghost of tea.

"So you'll trance yourself without a drug, and get into Ghyste Mortua. And then you'll destroy Ghyste Mortua," said Sable, "like all the other ghost-killers were going to. But they never managed it, did they, eh? What's *your* idea?"

"Wait and see."

Parl Dro wondered then if she could see, past the iron, the steel, the self-denying, cynical, adamant desire to kill the dead which symbolized his existence so bleakly, see by all that to the somber terror in his heart, lying there immovable as Myal on the bed.

Myal Lemyal did not know his body lay miles away under a sheet in a hovel. Myal's psychic body seemed as actual to him as actuality had ever seemed, and was even plagued by the same ills of nervousness and exhaustion. But then, the town of Tulotef seemed also actual. The town, and the girl.

And the three riders who had escorted them to the gate.

In the end, these men had not beaten Myal. They had not even let him ride the horse. At the last instant, as the irrevocable gateporch leaned over them—high, wide, echoing—they had pulled him down. As he landed on the paving, the instrument catching him again an almighty thump between the shoulders, a man had leapt for the vacant saddle. Spurs dug in, the horses shrilled. In a skirl of sparks and reverberant, gate-magnified hoofbeats, the riders dashed away into the heart of the unearthly town.

Myal rose, dabbing at fresh bruises. Ciddey Soban stood nearby. She was so completely normal, and mortal, that he caught his breath again in a whirling doubt of all facts and fantasies. White, bad-tempered, her eyes blazing, she slashed the dank atmosphere in the gate with her cat's tongue.

"*Scum! Villains!*" And then a host of detrimental words Myal was vaguely shocked—though not astounded—she knew.

After delivering these epithets, she stood simmering, like any spoiled noble girl who had not got the masculine treatment she supposed was her right.

It all seemed so real. The hollow gate, wide open and unguarded, yet like a score of similar town gates Myal had gone in and out of. The angry female. The soft cool vapors of night. The gauzy sounds of people and action going on in the vicinity: hoofs, feet, metalware, voices, wheels and occasional bells; a dog barked somewhere, lusty and demanding. There was even a vague smell like baking bread—

The only wrong note was the half-mooned darkness. All

this clamor of an industrious town in the forenoon, carried on at midnight.

"As for you—"

Myal turned automatically. Ciddey Soban glared at him.

"Damn it," said Myal defensively, "what was I supposed to do? You're all ghosts."

"*Be quiet.*"

He quailed at the venom in her eyes, and said, fawningly, "Well, *they* were—"

"You offered me your protection," she snarled.

"Did I?"

"And you let them molest me, threaten me with a sword."

"And you wanted to lead me into town by a ribbon."

"That's all you're good for. Someone's lapdog."

"They'd have beaten me up, while you—"

"I'd have laughed."

"I think," said Myal, turning from the gateway, "I'll just—"

"No you won't. As a protector, you're ridiculous, but you're all I have. You'll stay with me. You, and that silly stringed instrument."

She walked in the gate. She was imperious. It would be simple to retreat, dodge away into the forest that stretched from the slope, pressed like a huge crowd against the causeway, rank on rank of bladed darkness which was trees. Simple to retreat. Or was it simple? Something which was more than the willpower of the ghost girl was enticing him toward that gate.

A sudden uncanny notion struck Myal, unformed yet menacing. He had remembered the way the riders had threatened him by the pool, stating the penalties for those who consorted with the deadalive. Of course, they had been threatening him. But the odd thing was, they had spoken many of the words as they stared at Ciddey. As if they were grinningly, nastily unsure which of the two, the girl or the musician, was the ghost.

And then again, why had they abruptly abandoned Myal to his own—or Ciddey's—devices at the gateway? As if he did not really matter to them. The undead needed the living to feed from, was that not Parl Dro's enduring philosophy? So why—

"Myal Lemyal, *will* you do as I say?"

Ciddey was glaring again, from the town side of the gate.

"Why should I?" Myal asked, obeying her.

Once he was in the town, a sense of total helplessness overcame him, not physical, but mental; not even truly unpleasant. Ciddey and Tulotef had got the better of him. Small surprise. He gave in.

Ghyste Mortua was not as he had been picturing in the part-assembled song. Not dusk. Not dim and shriveled. No fireflies. And yet, so strange.

The stone street inclined upward, narrow and closed in by houses with blind walls. It was pitch dark there, but somehow everything was visible, in a thousand shades of black, even the bricks or the stones. While over the tops of roofs the gust of light dazzled into the sky, dousing the stars, which he had taken to be the light of the lamps of Tulotef—or was it rather the light of Tulotef *itself*? A glow like phosphorous on a bone. Myal braced himself to shudder, and the shudder did not come.

The sound was curious too, for noise was everywhere, yet no figures were directly apparent. Then, suddenly, gazing at a blank yard, you saw a man definite as your own hand seen by daylight. A cobbler mending a shoe, a smith hammering. Or two children playing with a cat.

Ciddey was prowling ahead of him, and he, dutiful page or bodyguard, or dog, or whatever he was supposed to be, remained about a respectful yard behind her. A large building blocked the head of the street, but with an arch through and a flight of steps. The first lamp burned in the arch, and Myal regarded it warily. It was a ghost lamp, for certain, a pale greenish-lemon moth light fluttering quietly in its smoky glass, clear and evident as a flower or a jewel in the gloom. And yet casting no brightness and no color from itself on anything. Not on the wall, not on the stair. Not even on Ciddey as she passed under. Nor on Myal. And when he held his hand against it, no blood showed in his fingers, and he felt no warmth.

"Come on," she snapped, ten steps above him. "Don't play with that. If you must play, play the instrument."

"No," he said stubbornly.

He followed her up the steps and she flounced haughtily ahead of him again. They emerged on a platform and beheld all the town spilled down the hill, about three quarters of a mile of it. There were towers, as the story said, slim and tall,

with crenellated baskets of stone at their tops. Alleys wound
and roofs overlapped each other in slaty scales. Everything
was lightless yet dotted by yellowish swarms of lamps, and
everything was also apparent in enormous detail, as if illu-
mined by a cool black sun of vast radiance. Beyond Tulotef,
the drama of the landscape. The star-channeled lake was
opened by the moon, or by the supernatural effulgence of the
town, a plate of silver chains, flickering, winking, as if under
the flare of a midsummer noon—and yet colorless. The same
occult rays hit the blades of distant mountains which rose
from the forest beyond. White as winter they were, as
described. And the forest was a black snow which had
carpeted the rest of the earth.

The country was silent as—yes, as the grave. But the grave
itself banged and sang and labored, cascades of noise flower-
ing up from the streets below. And now that he looked, Myal
could see a colossal procession winding through the broad
lower thoroughfares. Flatly red-winged torches, the stagnant
flash of brazen vessels giving off a gray-gold shine, as if in a
picture, light without *light*. There were priests in the con-
course, women in gowns of silver tissue, perhaps the lord of
the town himself. Bells rattled the night off their clappers and
out of their pear-shaped sound boxes.

"I'm cold," said Ciddey Soban.

"Are you?"

"Yes. Won't you play? The duke or the earl of Tulotef
might hear you. You could be a court musician."

"I've been that. It didn't suit me. I—had to leave."

"You weren't good enough."

"I was too good," said Myal mournfully. "The only thing I
can do well, and I do it too well, and everyone hates me."

"Please play for me, Myal."

"No."

"I command you. I am a Soban. You're just riffraff, a vag-
abond. Do it. Play!"

"I can't."

"Why not."

"I don't know."

Suddenly someone jostled Myal. He and the girl were
thrust together. There was a big crowd on the platform. They
had been there all the time, unnoticed, or else they had just
evolved. They were now completely real and three-dimen-

sional, they even smelled human—leather, sweat, scent, wine. Their object was to view the great procession choking its way through the streets.

"Mind yourself," someone said to Myal.

Someone else trod on his foot and hurt him.

Ciddey lay shivering on his chest.

With a slow dim panic, he realized that bodies pressed in his back where the instrument should have been. He felt stupidly across himself for the frayed embroidered sling, and it was not there.

He must have set the instrument down and forgotten to take it up. No, absurd. What then? He had only *imagined* he had brought it with him from the ridge? But he had experienced its weight. It had actually slammed into him two or three times. Why then had he replied he could not play it?

The crowd seemed to exist, but had not a moment ago.

The instrument did not exist any longer, but had.

Ghosts' concepts. The wills and beliefs and fancies of—ghosts.

Ciddey clung to him, pulling down his head toward her face. Jammed in the crowd, he kissed her, his mind wandering around and around behind his closed eyes.

"Parl Dro will follow you," she whispered, digging her long nails into his arms. "And bring the instrument with him."

"Maybe. Yes. I can't tell."

"He will." She smiled at him like a wolf. Then, as once before, she grew appallingly defenseless. "Look after me," she moaned.

A heavy man leaned on Myal drunkenly. Somewhere another girl in the crowd was whispering of a potion she had made to entice a man to come to her. Myal found, inadvertently almost, he had lifted the drunken man's money bag from his mantle. Ghost money. What did it matter?

They sought an inn, the way travelers might be expected to in an unknown town. The sign was richly painted, its colors shades of pallor, brass and dragon's blood. In the picture, a maiden held a unicorn helpless by its horn as a warrior in mail sheared off its head. Myal grimaced at it. Near the inn, the usual stream ran down the street. A cat carved of marble sat on one of the stepping stones, and Myal tried to pet it before he realized.

Men sat drinking at the inn tables. Lights burned and a fire, none of them giving glow or heat to the big room, only a hellish localized motion. An innkeeper came, and the thief paid for a room with his stolen money. Ciddey swept up the stair like a great lady. They ordered neither food nor drink. Like the lights of Tulotef, sustenance would be phantasmagorical and unnecessary. And on the stair, Myal asked himself: "The three riders gave me a drink. Or did I imagine it? Ghost-pretend. Surely I'm hungry?" But he was not, and he knew why not. He had died. The dead had killed him. It hadn't been a faint, but death. Then they had brought him here as a jest. And if Parl Dro came after him, Myal would have to be properly scared, like any other ghost confronted by an adept and professional ghost-killer.

Of course, all returning deadalive must have a link. Myal knew what his must be. The instrument. Which was very bizarre, because Ciddey—

"Don't suppose," she said, as they entered the room, "that we'll share this bed. The incident in the wood was a game. I wouldn't come near you normally. You can have the chair. By rights you should sleep on the floor, dog."

The bed had curtains like a black crow's wings. The narrow window stared toward the lake. The procession still glided by, two streets below. It had gone on and on, for almost two hours. Assuming, of course, it was at all possible to reckon time here. The moon had moved, however. Perhaps it was. Myal peered in the bloodless fire, and wondered why he was not gibbering with terror and despair.

"I'm cold," said Ciddey from the large black bed. She held out to him her small narrow hand. He was not afraid of her, either, nor did he want her any more. But he went to her, and presently got into the bed with her. They kissed and clung, in a sad, lazy, sensual nothingness. She murmured at his ear, "Cilny would be jealous. My sister would hate me, in bed with a man." Then, miles of deep and delicious and passionless kisses later: "You mustn't try to have me. I'm a virgin."

Obviously she had died a virgin, she could not lose her virginity after death. But he felt only the sort of dislocated concupiscence that came in fever dreams, and was unable to, or undesirous of, acting on it. In a dreary way, the sexual limbo was very pleasant. Certainly he did not want to stop embracing her, just as he did not want to intensify the embraces.

Then, languidly, between the long, long, purposeless kisses, they began to talk.

"I think I'm dead," he said. "I really must be."

"Ssh. Don't. Kiss me. You're not dead."

"But that's—mmm—yes, that's how I know. But I want to ask you—"

"No. Don't ask me. Kiss."

"Yes. Oh Ciddey. . . . I want to ask you about the musical instrument. About the link."

"Myal. . . ."

"It's my link to life. And Parl Dro's got it. And he's coming here because—well, because I just suppose he's a ghostkiller and he's obsessed with Tulotef, so he'll have to come here. But why you?"

"Why? Darling—"

"Darling. Why is the instrument your link, too?"

"So clever. Myal Lemyal's so clever. And so lovely."

"Ciddey—I wish you'd tell me."

"I will. You're only riffraff, but I love you. There, I've told."

"Dro burnt your shoe. And there was nothing else I had that could have been yours. I don't see how the instrument my father murdered a man to get can have anything to do with you. But it does. I was your energy source to get back, and your hatred of Dro was your motive. But the instrument was the link."

"So clever. How did you know? Ah—"

"Oh—I played a song to you on it in my sleep, and you arrived. When I played it backwards you went away. And when I went with you into the wood, I took it with me, or I thought I did. And when we were here, you wanted it played. When you realized it was an illusion, you were afraid—"

"Stop it. I don't want to discuss it. Kiss me."

"Yes . . . Ciddey? Let's stop pretending we're alive. It can't hurt if we tell the truth to each other."

"I love you."

"I love you, too. Only I'll wish I hadn't said it now. Because I don't. At least—"

"Myal—"

For a long while then there was just the mandragora kisses. The pulse of the unwarm fire in the grate casting neither shadow nor light, the gems of torches and lamps on the window similarly unconductive. The drowned noise of bells.

They might melt into the bed. They might freeze and become a gray statue, forever kissed together. He did not mind. Then she said, her voice small and thin as her little hands locked on his back: "When Dro comes, we must be strong and fight him. If you promise you'll help me fight him, I'll tell you. If you'll help me kill him. Will you? For my sister's sake."

It did not seem a huge thing to kill Parl Dro. It seemed a depressing thing, a vile thing, but quite possible.

"If I say yes, I may not mean it."

"When I—when I . . . after the stream . . . you would have killed him then."

"I was sick."

"Promise."

They writhed slowly, and he promised her, from some dark dungeon-deep ecstasy, and he did not mean it. And then she told him, like a trusting child, about the instrument, puzzling him a great deal, so he questioned her awhile, between the long rollers of their deadalive and timeless and unimperative love.

There were really two very atrocious aspects on which his recognition foundered. And in the end, when he was convinced, he felt ridiculous. Even as a ghost. A couple of the idiotic and perverse mainstays of his life were gone. But since he was dead, maybe that was only right.

By then, something peculiar was beginning to happen in the room.

It originated at the window, and was a sort of steady drawing, a bleeding away of substance. Myal became, for the first time since realizing his condition, nervous.

"What is it?" he demanded. Then he understood without getting an answer from the girl. They both reacted quite intuitively, falling apart like two tired pages in a book. And they lay, the lovers, in the tomb of the bed, watching the manifestation of dawn at the window.

It was not like any dawn he had witnessed when alive. It had neither color nor light. It simply sucked the world away, consumed it, in an invisible conflagration.

"What happens," Myal said eventually, "to us?"

"What do you mean?"

"In the daylight."

"Oh, day's unimportant."

He was frightened, and lay rigid by her listlessness, waiting to lose consciousness. True, he had heard of ghosts who moved about by day, just as he had told Parl Dro, but they were rare, perhaps eccentric. Night was the canvas the dead-alive required. Certainly the town of Tulotef required it.

The room was like a vague sketch. The bed was a billow of dark mist. And Ciddey—she turned on her side as if to sleep, and dissolved. And as this happened, for a moment, he thought he saw a fish leap through her hair.

With his horror ready, Myal glanced at his own body, and was astonished to find it still opaque. Surely by now his awareness should be fading out.

The last of the room went suddenly, like a swath of smoke blowing off the hill. He glimpsed the revolting inn sign whirling in the wide air like a cumbersome bird. And then the mattress under him was rock, and the fires of dawn broke through abruptly into his sight, blinding him with their mortal violence.

CHAPTER ELEVEN

All the colors in the spectrum raced, like an enraged mob, over the hill, trampling through Myal's eyes. He felt he could not stand it, after the murks and smolders and quarter tones of the Ghyste. He also felt a keen insecurity at being left behind. The night had pulled out from shore, like a huge boat laden with its passengers, and somehow he had missed it. Was he then, incredibly, still quick? No. For trying to pick up a pebble on the slope, his perfectly fleshy-looking hand went through it. And when the sun was higher, he got up, having selected a stunted little tree that had apparently been poking through the canopied bed all night, unnoticed, and he walked at it, and, with a desolate wretchedness, right through it.

With a cry of fear, he stood and listened to his heart pounding where there was no heart to pound. He supposed if he stopped believing in his heart, it would stop beating, and hastily he tried to avoid that ultimate loss. He glanced around wildly in an effort to distract himself. And was duly distracted by the bare hillside of sere pallid grass and weather-burnished rock, naked among the thousand black fur backs of the forest which framed it. There was no town anywhere by day. Not even rubble, not even the scars of the great landslip remained. Everything that had been had dropped into and beneath the lake. Then he looked inadvertently down toward the shore, caught his breath—unnecessarily, kidding himself like all ghosts—and swore.

The broad waters of the star-rayed lake were gone. There was only a sprawl of chasm, arid, eroded mud that was hardening into stone, from which five bleak gulleys ran away.

Myal leaned out from the empty hill, staring. Like a big well, the lake had gone dry. Either the river had failed it at its source, or some internal plug had been pulled. Thirty years or more, the bed had been drying out. The night waters of Tulotef were also a ghost. But what of the tumbled town which had, in all the myths, rumors or tales, lain on its floor?

"Pretty, isn't it?" said Parl Dro's softly articulate, unmistakable voice, about ten feet behind him.

Myal attempted to spin around, lost his balance, skidded down the hill. He ended on one knee, clawing at the turf he could not actually grasp.

Dro watched him. Black mantle, black hair, black eyes against the scald of blue sky. Impassive. Myal's musical instrument hung by its sling across his black shoulder.

Myal grimaced.

"Well, get on with it."

Dro raised both eyebrows.

"I mean," said Myal, angry in his fright, "I'm here. You're here. You've got the link—my link—the instrument. So destroy it. Get rid of me. What the hell's keeping you?"

Dro's long eyebrows leveled like the death black eyes under them. There was no playful cruelty at all in his face.

"You seem to be very sure of my next move."

"I should be. I've listened to enough of your damned boasting. Pull out the dead like rotten teeth. The deadalive must die. I'm not fighting you. Get on with it."

"How convenient for me, professionally speaking," said Dro, "that you happen to be one of those unusually strong-willed, witch-gifted ghosts who are able to manifest in broad daylight."

"Look," said Myal shivering, wondering bewilderedly how he was able to, "I'm a coward, right? And what I really can't bear is waiting around for something awful to happen. So will you please do it now? Or is this what makes you feel good? Sadistically terrorizing the dead."

"You're not dead."

"Just," said Myal. He paused. "What?"

"You are not dead."

"Ha," said Myal. He smashed his hand through a rock. "Look. See? I'm dead."

"You're out of your body, but your body's alive. You can go back to it eventually. Not necessarily inspiring, but a fact."

"Shut up," said Myal. He put his face in his hands. "I always said you were a bastard."

"So far as I know, I was conceived inside wedlock. Your own situation may be a little more complex."

"Shut up."

"Remember Cinnabar? The kind redhead who loaned you a horse?"

"The kind redhead who loaned you her——"

"She gave you a clay dog which you put in your shirt pocket. There was a drug in the dog which soaked out and into you. A drug to induce cataleptic trance."

"To induce *what*?"

"The life activities of the body are slowed to the minimum, and the astral state can then be triggered. It seems Cinnabar thought you psychically capable enough to release your own astral persona voluntarily, under the right conditions. But not adept enough to produce the trance unaided."

"You've got me all confused," shouted Myal.

"Which is, of course, extremely difficult to do."

Myal stood up. He looked at the ground.

"I'm alive—somewhere."

"In an old woman's decrepit hovel, about seven or eight miles from here."

"That sounds cozy."

"She'll take care of you, till you're able to get back."

"When will *that* be?"

"When the drug wears off. And when you're finished here."

"If I go to a tree, I walk through it," said Myal. "Why don't I sink through the ground?"

"Basic common sense. Probably even your limited perspective can see it would be rather pointless."

"In other words, you don't know."

"In other words," said Parl Dro, "you can be incorporeal, but only as far as you want to be. You can walk through a stone wall and pick up a plate on the other side. A moment's adjustment of willpower is all that's necessary." He drew the instrument off his shoulder and held it between his hands by its two peculiar necks. Then he raised the instrument and slung it at Myal. "Catch."

Myal leapt forward, not thinking, guided by a vision of smashed wood and broken ivory. He caught the instrument just before it touched the earth. It was solid and heavy in his arms, the wires vibrating quietly like a cat purring. It did not slip through him. He held it and his legs buckled.

"A practical demonstration is often more effective than a lecture," said Dro. He sat down on the hillside, straightening out the crippled left calf, and Myal saw the black eyes momentarily go blind with pain.

Myal sat on a jut of rock, the instrument on his knees. He rubbed the garishly painted wood, fascinated, his fingers caressing, as they had always bodily done, the ivory chips sunk in there.

"You're sure," he eventually said, "I'm alive?"

"I'm sure."

"Cinnabar was crazy."

"Not quite. The story goes that if you'd got into Tulotef physically, they'd have served you for dinner."

"She thought she was helping, pushing me in this way? Because of my song I wanted to make—"

"I'm afraid she thought she was helping me," Parl Dro said. He looked out toward the dry mud chasm of the dead lake.

"You called it Tulotef," said Myal.

"Yes."

"According to you, that's supposed to be unwise, isn't it?"

"Yes."

A melancholy oppression of anticlimax lay over Myal. He traced the patterns on the instrument, but felt no inclination to play it. A silence widened between them. The whole earth was silent where the ghostly clangor of the town had been before. A light wind flapped over the hill and brushed the tops of the forest, but it made hardly any sound, only the sound of emptiness. Even the resins of the forest did not smell so high up, or else the uncanny spot had sucked its perfumes away, eating the life force of the trees, the hill, the land, as it ate the life force of living men who wandered, or were coerced, inside the gates.

"I spent the night," Myal said at last, "with Ciddey Soban. We didn't—I don't want you to think—"

"I'm not thinking anything."

"All right. But she told me. The link that's keeping her on earth. If I tell you, I want your word you won't harm her."

"Harm?"

"Won't throw her out of this world. Not until she's ready."

"You can guess what my word is worth."

"I'll trust you."

"No, you don't trust me. Something's puzzling you, and you want to tell me so it will puzzle you less. That's all. And you're prepared to betray Ciddey Soban to me for that."

"She wants to kill you."

"She shouldn't be strong enough yet to try."

"She's very strong. She's used your energy too, to draw on through me. A ghost-killer's life force must be particularly restorative for a ghost. And she was a witch, too."

"You underestimate your own psychic force. She didn't need me. And you don't get my word."

Myal gnawed a blade of grass he had found he was after all able to pluck.

"I'll tell you anyway. I still have the advantage. You'll see why."

"Because presumably," said Dro, "Ciddey's link is located on that instrument I just handed back to you."

Myal frowned, thunder stolen.

"You're so intelligent. Know where?"

"I'd thought about the inset ivory," said Dro, "but so far as I know, she never lost any bones."

"Not a bone," said Myal. "A tooth. A milk tooth. She fell as a baby, and it got knocked out. She was just a year old."

Myal took another deep breath that was pointless. The absurdity of the story upset him, how two of the guidelines of his life had rested on lies.

"Old Soban kept Ciddey's tooth. Superstitition. Then he had a chance to sell something. He was always trying to sell things, heirlooms, furniture, for drink. He was a drunkard, like my sot of a father. That's probably how they met. In some inn. Didn't care about being landowner mixing with traveling rubbish, then, drinking each other under the stinking table. Then Soban got my bloody stink of a father interested in buying a unique musical instrument. It came from some foreign country. No one could play it. That was true enough. My drunken boss-eyed father went to Soban's house, took one look at the instrument, and thought he, being a genius, could master it, and make a fortune. He'd get ideas like that sometimes. So he felt the instrument over, businesslike, and plunked away on the wires, and blew down the reed. And then he said he'd buy it, but there was a bit of ivory missing out of the inlay. What'd Soban take off the asking price?"

"To which," said Dro, staring at the lake, "Soban replied he could replace the ivory. And he took the thing upstairs and got the milk tooth and rammed it into the wood where the hole was."

"That's it. Ciddey knows, because her father made a great history out of it. She said it shamed her. Till I came back on the same road my father did, and it turned out so useful for her."

"But there's more," said Dro.

"Yes. There's this big joke. I suppose it *is* fairly funny. Soban had a trick. He used to get bits of things, and weld them or carpenter them together. The instrument . . ." Myal clutched suddenly and convulsively at the two wooden necks resting against him. ". . . the instrument was like that, too, you see. He got two stringed bodies—guitars, mandolins, something, and carved them up and then joined them together. And the reed he threw in as an afterthought, to make it more—more bizarre. The joke was, nobody was *meant* to be able to play the damn thing. Nobody *should* be able to play it. And my father used to smash me from one end of the wagon to the other, when he was drunk, learning me how he'd teach me when he was sober."

"And you can, of course, play it exquisitely."

"It makes me sick. It really does. And the other thing."

"Which is?"

"My bloody father. How he used to sit over it, polishing the wood and twanging the wires, and say he'd killed the man who'd owned the instrument. He never killed Ciddey's father for it. He never even *stole* it. He *paid* for it."

"Which disappoints you,"

"No. It's just—I based my life on my screaming fear of his violence, on his capacity for murder, maybe. And he didn't. Which is odd, because he looked like he meant it when he said it."

Dro got up. Myal glanced at him. Dro said slowly, "Do you remember what he actually said?"

"The exact words? Yes, I do. He said them often enough."

"Say them."

Myal twisted uncomfortably, reacting to an insidious tremor of tension on the air. A tension which had been there all along, of course, which was now growing, swamping both of them.

Finally, Myal looked down and touched the strings. Perhaps unconsciously, astral or not, he switched himself over into his past, over into the skin of that hated, terrible man, whose minstrel's hands had clamped on the instrument, whose small pig's eyes had congealed in a cold red blankness. Savoring, tasting what had been, what he had done.

"He used to say," said Myal, " 'You learn to play this, you ugly cretinous little rat. I killed a man because of this. I killed him good and dead.' "

"Yes," Dro said.

His own eyes were wide open, but they looked shut. Like the eyes of a man who has just died.

Myal's father's image slid off from Myal. He surfaced from it, sighing, as if coming up from deep water.

"What is it?" he said to Dro.

"It's a dry lake," said Parl Dro. "And we're going down there."

"*What?*"

Parl Dro began to walk away, picking down over the slope, the wrecked leg swinging itself with a stiff, agonized elegance.

Bemused, Myal scrambled, forgetting that no incorporeality need ever scramble, after him.

The shelves of the lake were hard-baked, already partly petrified, composing a terraced effect of powdery stone, like the earthworks of some extraordinary, inverted castle. Here and there, the antique slimes and marshes the lake had tried to transform itself into as it emptied, had grown weird trees and thickets which, in turn, had perished and calcified. It did not seem to be only the going of the water, however, which had made the place so inimical to what tried to live there. Probably the upheaval in the hill which had slain living Tulotef, was also responsible for the draining of the lake. There had been laval activity deep down to complement the earth-shake above. As a result, some fluid poison or other, some literal scum of the earth, had processed itself into the waters of the lake. So that, as it died, it also killed.

There was nothing beautiful anywhere, nothing to resemble the beauty of a ruin. Even the beauty of a wilderness or a waste was absent. Close to, more than anything, the corpse of the lake and its vitrified channels looked like some horrid amateur sculpting in river clay, set in the sun, and then magnified beyond all belief and all reason.

It was a couple of hours' climb down to the topmost shelves. Then they walked about there for a couple of hours, or glumly sat, staring into the abyss, not speaking. It was like a mouth into hell, with none of hell's hellish glamor, not even the warmth of flames.

Later, they went out along a cracked dancing floor of natural brick, observing the sticky shadows that still stuck to the river bottom. Those inadequate waters had been poisoned too. You saw the bones of fish lying thick as fallen leaves, ribbed into the petrifying mud far below. Mval noted that the forest, where it touched the edges of the lake and its channels, was also dying. Dead trees stood nude, like fishbones grown to great heights. There were no birds, and no beasts on the ground.

Nowhere was there any sign of the Tulotef which, the landslide behind it, had poured away into the lake.

They sat on a fallen tree as the afternoon began to come, stringing out their shadows artistically on panes of sun.

"Where is it, then?" asked Myal. It was the first thing either of them had said, beyond occasional invective, for hours. The conversation on the hill above loomed over them, but they had left it there, convincingly inaccessible as the grass, till they should climb back. Myal carried the instrument in the old way. He could no longer walk through things, as if the instrument, being solid. prevented him.

"If you mean the town," said Dro, "you're looking at it."

"No, I'm not. If the lake's gone. there should be a ruin lying down there, exposed. Broken roofs and snapped vertebrae."

"They're there. You can't see them because either the weather and the water's all but rotted them away, or they're changing into stone along with the banks."

"Oh." Myal picked up a handful of loose flints, glad he could, and tossed them over into the smear of liquid in the river. They struck with turgid little plops, or cracking sounds where they did not reach the water and rapped fish spines instead. The cold white crags beyond the forest stared at the blue sky. The only live thing seemed to be the sky. Myal did not look back at the hill where he had lain most of the night, with his astral body plastered to Ciddey Soban. "I deduce," said Myal, "you've got some outrageously sagacious plan for destroying them. I mean what's left of the ruins."

"No."

Myal shifted, looking at Dro warily.

"But they're the psychic link for Tul—for the Ghyste, aren't they? You have to destroy them."

"The key to releasing the ghost is to change the link. Metamorphosis. The bone has to be smashed. The shoe has to be burnt."

"Well how are you going to burn and smash all that?"

Dro looked back at him. He appeared older than any line in his face, and charismatic as a gaunt black cat.

"I'm not, Myal. I don't have to. Most of it's been changed already. Most of it's crumbled or ossified. That's sufficient. And what hasn't, soon will. Another couple of winters' snows, another hot summer, and there won't be any link left here that Tulotef's collective ghost can hold on to."

"Wait a minute."

Dro gazed at him with enormous courtesy.

"I was up there," said Myal. "It was real. They're strong in—up there. A whole busy town, and men looking as lifelike as you."

"Or you," said Dro.

Myal looked slightly uncomfortable.

"Are you going to explain?"

"Yes, I'll explain."

Dro spoke carefully and steadily, watching Myal. Myal could not always meet the older man's gaze. There were about fifteen years between them in age, but it felt like a century. It felt like a hurt, a wound that had never healed and never would.

Tulotef had appeared strong and whole to Myal because he had expected it to be, and because he himself was no longer inside the fleshy envelope of mundane human life. The streets, the crowds, the great procession; the man he had robbed, the innkeeper, the bed—even the three riders and their horses in the wood—everything had been there, but where he, and for that matter dead Ciddey, had seen facts there had been only echoes.

"It's the stories that are strong, that have got stronger, even as Ghyste Mortua itself has decayed. The stories Cinnabar believed, after her man started playing with magic and ran off with someone else. The stories you hear told all over this end of the country. Yes, the ghosts have got more irrepressible year by year—in legend. In reality, they're just a few papers left blowing about in the woods, and on the hill."

Dro told Myal about Sable in the forest, living so near the Ghyste.

"She frequently sees the ghosts of the Ghyste. They've grown solid. She anticipated seeing them even by day. But that was because she reckoned on seeing them that way. Or wanted to, and imagined it, for all I know. The giveaway was that she lived close enough to have been easy prey, if they could take her. In the tales, Tulotef abducts any live human in the vicinity to feed off his energy. Cinnabar's belief again. And mine, long ago, when I studiously learned how to project my spirit out of my body, in order to come in safely at their gate. No. They're harmless now to the living. The only victim they can seize on is someone who couldn't be a victim at all, someone in the same state as themselves. Or near it. Ciddey, or you."

"But," said Myal.

He fell silent, remembering how the persons in the town had sometimes been there, sometimes not. Remembering the aimless repetitive activities. Even the three bullies in the wood, who had dragged him from the pool, had seemed to appear out of nowhere. And their grisly jibes about necrophilia between mortal and deadalive, their turning from Ciddey to him and back again—as if the two new ghosts were so fresh, so vital by comparison, the riders might be mistaking one, or both, for the genuinely *living*.

"But," said Myal again, "you thought, or you wouldn't have come here."

"When I started out, I had good reason to credit a malevolent, sorcerous ghost town at the peak of its powers. Then, to reach here became a compulsion. It was a place I had to get to. But I've suspected, over the past days of traveling, what I might find."

"Didn't sound like it."

"No."

"So what will you do?"

"Let it finish dying on its own. It already practically has."

"That doesn't sound like a ghost-killer talking."

"It isn't, anymore."

Myal went cold. He was not sure why. He stared at Dro, and now Dro smiled and looked away.

"So you needn't worry about the only real ghost left here. I mean Ciddey," said Dro. "I'm afraid her sister didn't escape my vengeful headlong zeal. Which is maybe just as well. But Ciddey . . . she can be your problem."

"Thank *you*. You said she'd feed off me."

"Maybe she won't. I've realized something. It doesn't always happen that way, or not permanently. She's already manifested out of your vicinity, in Cinnabar's village street. When Ciddey's strong enough, she may always be able to maintain herself, without—" Dro broke off.

"This isn't you talking," Myal said.

Dro stood up again and walked off. Myal got up and followed. Halfway back along the natural brick dancing floor, Dro turned.

"Why don't you go and write your damned song?"

"Or, put it another way, get lost."

"What a talent you're developing for words, Myal Lemyal."

"It's being with you," Myal snapped back. "It rubs off. I'll start limping next."

"All right," said Dro. "I've seen you physically housed. I've told you you can get back into your body. I've explained Tulotef. What else do you want?"

"You think *explaining* is enough? *Telling* is enough? I want some proof."

"What proof?"

"Wait till nightfall. Then meet me in the town. Just as you are, without any bloody trance like the one your redhead dumped me in without a may I or a shall I. Flesh and blood, a reformed ghost-killer. In Ghyste Mortua after sunset. Safe."

Something ran over Parl Dro's face.

"I decline."

"You're afraid."

"Yes. Probably. But not of what you think."

"I'm not thinking. My mind's a blank."

Dro said nothing, not even the inevitable retort.

"After sunset," Myal repeated. He struck a pose, and did not feel foolish doing so. "If I'm still there," he announced, "I've got a feeling you have to be."

"Your magnetic personality," said Dro. He was recovering.

"Not quite. But it occurs to me you either come after me or leave me enough help so that I can follow you, one way or another."

"Which must mean I need you for something."

"Right."

"I wonder what it could possibly be."

"Cinnabar knew."

"Cinnabar probably supposed you were my fancy boy."

Myal took half a step back.

"And I suppose that's what *you* think it is, too."

"What is?"

"The fact that I—I'm drawn—that I—" Myal blushed, and very painfully. He turned, scooped up another flint and hurled it at the hill of Tulotef where once the flints had crashed on uplifted faces in a deadly rain. His body lay in a hovel eight miles away, yet the astral body could still burn with embarrassment. Or seem to, feel as if it did. "I'll see you up there in the town after sunset," said Myal. He strode away toward the hill, leaving Dro standing still as if ossifying along with the lake, the land, the bones of the fish.

A few minutes after the sun had submerged, carelessly smudging the horizon, Ciddey Soban found herself lying in a great bed, under a raven-wing canopy, alone.

The smoke-pink shades of sunfall made no impression on the room. Dusk was identified by a solidifying of furnishings, walls, thoughts. Ciddey sat up in the tomb-cold sheets, and understood that Myal, who had been with her a moment ago—before the brief blending of day had interrupted them—was gone. And not only gone. The paranoia of her condition instantly overwhelmed her with the apprehension of bad news.

Parl Dro was in Tulotef, and Myal had gone to meet him.

Myal was Dro's accomplice. Apprentice, maybe.

And she, lonely and lowering herself, wrapped in the warm arms of Myal, had betrayed herself to him. She had felt a sinister joy as she told him. But she had been unwise.

Stupid to think the dead were a fraternity. Myal would be loyal to his master, Dro. Even in death, Myal would stand beside Dro, against her.

Ciddey beheld her sister's lovely childish face floating bloated in water. That was why Ciddey kept dreaming she herself was dead. Identifying herself with Cilny. Foolish. Ciddey was not dead. The well, the stream—no, she was alive. It was Myal who was dead. Myal who had made her come with him to this strange town.

The day had gone so quickly. Why could she not remember it?

Somewhere, music played on the streets, and bells began tenderly to gild the darkness. A drop of blanched almond yellow hung in the window, slid away, was replaced by another. Ciddey recalled the procession in which the town's duke, or earl, would be riding.

Defenseless and alone, and well-born, she must appeal to him for protection. The murderer could not touch her then. Indeed, she might ask for vengeance. Dro had killed her sister. Yes, she had pursued him to exact payment for that. And now she would. She *must*.

She flung herself from the bed and ran through the closed door, not noticing, and down the curiously deserted stairs of the inn, on to the black-lit streets.

CHAPTER TWELVE

———◦◦————————◦◦———

The procession blew down the wide street. The lamps and candles hung from it like pale fruits, but it came like a long wave of somber weather, a dark wind. The priesthood wore dull crimson habits and dull gold cowls, tarnished as if under water. Censers smoked and imparted an oily fragrance. Boys in livid white sang in high voices above the bells. A carriage passed behind funeral horses with stained-glass eyes, then another, and another. The earl or duke rode among armed mailed men. A greenish storm of cloaks swirled about them.

Where the wide street led into another a flight of broad stairs came down from an upper thoroughfare. Ciddey stood on the stairs, holding herself upright, waiting.

As the priests and the carriages unfurled, she tossed away her hair, combing it with her fingers. When she saw the mailed men, she searched their ranks, looking for her assailants of the previous night. But she found it hard, nearly impossible to recall their individual appearances. Within the processional crowd every face looked blurred. Even the face of the duke-earl, riding in his rich regalia among his men. He was expressionless, his features like old embroidery in a faded tapestry.

Nevertheless: "My lord!" Ciddey cried out, raising her small fists. "I beg your mercy! My lord, hear me!"

And then, in a terrible series of moments, she became aware the procession was unhaltable, that she was to be ignored. She felt both panic and bruised ego. She uttered a scream of frustration and flung herself off the stair against the nearest horse.

For a second, she could not seem to catch hold of it, could not even seem to feel it. Then her senses came clear, and she clung to a mane, and to a booted leg. Looking up, she recognized after all the face of one of the bravos from the wood.

"Sir," she called, "I beg you. Please listen to me."

The man looked down, and gradually seemed to see her, as if he revived from a strange insomniac sleep. But if he remembered their former dealings he gave no signal. He tried to thrust her away.

"Sir," she wailed, "I'm well-born. I need to speak to your lord. I must *warn* him. He's in danger."

"Oh yes," said the mailed rider. A red jewel dazzled gruesomely, as it had beside the pool when he had lifted the broadsword to slash at her. As it had when the sword had somehow, miraculously, done her no harm. "They all say that. Let me speak to the lord, they say. Just five minutes. We have penalties for obstruction here."

Insanely, clinging to the horse and to his leg, she was being pulled backward, borne away with the procession. The rider had stopped trying to dislodge her. He leered at her.

"You don't understand. Someone's coming to your town. He's a murderer. He'll kill us all."

"Up you come," said the rider, and hauled her onto the saddle in front of him. He had done that last time, too. Did he really not recall? "I might kill him first," he said.

"Yes," she said, "I'd like that."

"What else do you like?"

"Let me speak to your master."

"You're a newcomer. You can't speak to the duke."

"I'm Ciddey. Don't you recall me?"

"This is Tulotef. I can't recall every girl I've nodded to on the street."

It was curious. The man seemed to have grown more positive, more human, the more she talked to him. And the riders around her were also less indefinite. They were laughing together now, or staring about, with hauteur. The horses snorted. Even the bells sounded more intense. Ciddey tried to turn her head, but the rider cuffed her. A sentence rose to her lips, and she could no longer deny it, though she shied from its meaning as she said it.

"The man who is coming here. His name is Parl Dro. Have you ever been told what—*a ghost-killer is?*"

An extraordinary thing happened. She had spoken softly, yet her words seemed to intensify as they left her mouth. They blossomed, spread, enveloped the street, hitting the walls of the houses, the stunned sky, like frightened birds thrown from an opened cage. And all at once, the unhaltable procession had halted. It appeared to petrify. The riders sitting bolt upright, the horses' heads reared forward. The choir of boys' voices died away just as the bells fell quiet, as if a wind had dropped.

Ciddey trembled, or she felt she did. And then, behind her, that man with the tapestry face coming unstitched spoke aloud.

"Bring her here to me."

Ciddey's rider turned his horse smartly and shouldered back through the stylized tableau. No one looked at them. If an eye blinked, a tassel fluttered, a bead gleamed, she might only have imagined it. There was no noise in all the town.

The duke of Tulotef sat and gazed at her.

"Who are you?"

"A Soban. Ciddey Soban."

"I've never heard the name."

She was suddenly icy cold, and lonely, lonely. Among strangers, without friends. There was no one to turn to after all.

"I wanted to warn you. A traveler is coming who is—"

"Yes," said the duke. He was like a rag doll. His face was all undone now, and he seemed ready to unravel from head to toe, and be rolled up into some other dimension.

She wanted to go home. She wanted not to be afraid, or in search of vengeance. No longer a heroine. She wanted obscurity, loss of identity, peace. She wanted an answer to some question she did not understand how to ask. But Myal— Myal and Parl Dro—

"You must destroy him. You've got the power. There are enough of you," she said bitterly, not really sure what she was bitter about, or talking about. "It's you or him. He's very accomplished at his *trade*. I've watched him at work. I *know*."

This man, this duke, had ruled in Tulotef on the night the hill fell on him.

When she drowned, he had already been returning to this place for centuries. She lowered her eyes. She tasted water, then ashes. She said again, "Destroy him."

When the sun had gone and the dead town began to come back it did not look quite as it had. The stone streets were less absolute. The tops of the towers were cloudy and the scalloping of the roofs below seemed bathed in a soft lake fog. For, of course, the lake had returned also, filling up its basin and its channels, as though the world bled water. Yet even the lake was subtly altered, as if it had frozen over in the late summer dusk, become a sheet of luminous, motionless ice. Myal observed these things and their difference to him almost impatiently. He felt an odd relaxation, because everything had become a farce. He, alive yet a spirit, standing in a ghost town with a real wooden instrument on his shoulder, the other shoulder resting on the corner of a phantom house that felt quite real also. In such a situation, either madness or sublime indifference would result. His temperament had automatically chosen the latter. So he leaned there, and watched the endless procession swim by down in the streets below, and even entertained the notion of improvising a melodic counterpoint to the bells and the songs, but somehow he never got as far as bringing the instrument forward where his fingers could reach the strings.

On an opposite wall there was some scribbled graffiti. Myal's limited education made him dismiss the fact he could not read it. Then he realized he could not read it because it was written mirror fashion, back to front.

He was waiting for Parl Dro—initially, with glib certainty, which masked a vague unease. After about half an hour, with a nervous agitation that masked alarm, rage and a curious unaccountable anguish.

Myal was not sure why he had demanded Dro's appearance in Tulotef. The argument he had given was dramatic and inane—*proof*. Proof of what, and who wanted it? No, Myal was conscious that he had merely been forcing the issue. And that, as from the very start of their acquaintance, if such it could be called, Myal had felt a foolish magnetism to Dro, one way or another. The magnetism worried Myal for a number of reasons. At first, it had seemed just another of his impulsively fatal fascinations with the element of danger. He had had, besides, the excuse of wanting to make a song of Ghyste Mortua. But when had that idea first taken hold of him? Could he really pin it down as being *before* he tried to rob the ghost-killer in the mountain valley village? It seemed to Myal now that there had been some faintly unsavory destiny that had directed him over the mountain pass and into the village, only four or five days before Parl Dro also limped the same way. Unsavory and supernatural. For not only had Myal's wandering advent meant a meeting with Dro, but also the ultimate revelation about the instrument—no longer a rare terpsichorean mystery, but a jest, a con trick, the toy of a clown. The coincidences that belabored the plot Myal's recent days seemed to have become niggled him. Dro and he, and Ciddey Soban come to that, seemed tangled like strands of wool.

Something unprecedented was happening to the procession. He had not been watching it with all his attention, but in retrospect, it seemed to have stopped, and now it seemed to be changing course like a demented river—

"Enjoying yourself?"

As before, Myal nearly overbalanced. He whirled around with a yell of startled vexation and of relief. Parl Dro stood under one of the yellow lamps, still as if carved. As on the hill, there had been no discernible prologue to his arrival.

"You like giving me heart failure, don't you," said Myal.

"Not particularly. It's too easy."

"Well, you're here."

"So I am. Now what do we do?"

"I—don't know," said Myal slowly. "I think we just wait. Something's going to turn up."

"Yes, something's bound to do that." Dro looked away over the slope to the muddled writhing of the procession. "You realize your psychic abilities," said Dro, "undisciplined and infantile as they are, have persuaded you to precipitate a crisis."

"Oh, don't give me that."

"I'm afraid that's exactly what I have given you."

The procession was spooling up into an alleyway. Myal was suddenly reminded of a flock of sheep, and let out a crow of laughter. The duke-earl of Tulotef, and all his ghoulish court, were coming this way. Insubstantial or not. Harmful or not. Certainly, a crisis.

On the road, they would pass by the inn where Myal and Ciddey had lain together. Maybe that was significant. He had noted the inn sign jutting out across the street between the roofs quite some way down. And though he could not see it, the girl would still be trapping the unicorn by its horn and the mailed warrior slashing off the unicorn's head. A castration symbol? Or maybe a simple omen. Myal turned back to Dro.

"I think Ciddey's with the procession. If so, she's said something about you to their ruler here—about your line of work. You said Tulotef was weak, but *how* weak is Tulotef's weak? They *could* kill you, could they?"

"Unless I was here in astral shape only, as you are. As I originally planned to be. As you dissuaded me from being, did you not?"

"I'm sorry. I thought—you said—"

"They don't kill. Not randomly any more. They haven't the energy left to do it, and there's no true incentive. Except with an exorcist. That hate goes as deep with the deadalive as fear of the deadalive goes with most humans."

Myal choked down presumably imaginary nausea, and said, "Get going. Run."

"*Run*? You forget I'm a cripple," said Dro very graciously.

"Well hobble then. I'll stall them."

"With what? Handstands? Communal singing?"

"I'll think of something. They can't hurt *me*. Can they?"

"Probably not. I wouldn't swear to it, under the circumstances."

"I know you've got a death wish," said Myal coldly. "Any kind of murderer has. But don't indulge it here and now. Go on."

"While you bravely fight them off. That's what it will come to."

"*Go.*"

"Have you ever fought the deadalive?"

"Will you—"

Parl Dro stood like an emperor, watching the tide of death

sweep around corners, between walls, up steps. Myal shouted at him, then muttered, then ceased communication of any sort. He too watched, with a fundamental sinking of his non-present vitals, until the crimson specters of Tulotef's priesthood brimmed up into the street, directly in front of him. Priests, a choir, even the carriages had somehow negotiated the route. Then everything folded aside, and a wedge of mailed riders came pushing through.

Myal saw through all of them. Not literally, since they appeared solid enough; their insubstantiality proclaimed itself in other, more insidious ways. Yet his eyes seemed to pierce them all, like any unknown mob, seeking and resting themselves on a single familiar face, which obviously was Ciddey's.

White as some wicked flower, she sat on a horse which a man in mail had been leading. His face was a blank, as if set there ready to be sketched in with emotion, personality. All their faces were the same. Except for hers.

There was also a man riding close at her side, clothed in an oddly faroff glitter. He must be the duke. Ciddey, not taking her eyes from Myal, made a small gesture to this man, deferring to him. Yet the duke of Tulotef hung there, somehow creditable only because Ciddey included him in her awareness.

And it was Ciddey who spoke.

"Hallo, traitor," she said to Myal. And then she called him a very foul name. Although Myal had been on the receiving end of it countless times, it unnerved him especially, coming from her kissable lips. But her eyes had gone past him. They had fixed on Parl Dro. "Lord duke," said Ciddey, "the man in black is the man I told you of. The murderer. He killed my sister virtually in front of me. My darling sister, all I had in the world. I swore to have justice from him. I dedicated myself to it. I came all these miles to your town and your court to ask it."

The ghost duke stared at Parl Dro. Some vestige of decayed mortal anger marked his countenance, which was firmer now. His long-nailed hands tensed very slightly on the jeweled reins.

"The lady has a grievance against you," said the duke to Parl Dro. "How are you prepared to answer it?"

"With a politely smothered yawn," said Dro.

"Your insolence suggests desperation."

"I'm sorry. It was meant to suggest boredom."

"I—" said the duke.

Ciddey cut through like a thin white blade.

"Don't debate with him, lord duke. Kill him." Ciddey leaned from the horse and clutched the shoulders of the mailed retainer who had led it. "You kill him."

The retainer tensed, given life. But, "How?" said the duke simply, over Ciddey's head.

Ciddey snarled. Her long teeth flashed silver. She had stopped being a girl. She had become what she truly was. The hair could not rise on Myal's astral scalp and neck, but nevertheless he felt if shifting. A movement smoothed over the crowd, also. A brief exploratory movement—testing itself—forward, toward Dro. And Myal could see in it a host of flickering hands, a thousand nails, like long flat blades—the nails that went on growing in a grave, those things of the body which, like the deadalive themselves, refused to acknowledge death. And, as if to complement Myal's observation, "How?" whispered Ciddey. "Why, just tear him in pieces."

Myal turned wildly. Parl Dro only stood there, not reacting in any fashion. Myal turned as wildly back again. Like the first chord of a hideous song, Ciddey ordered the crowd to follow her, by willpower and sheer hate. He had lain with that, comforting it and caressing it.

She slid from the horse and started to walk across to them, toward Dro. The crowd surged after, one gluey, mindless, malevolent step at a time.

As Myal moved, it was like plunging into a sea of ice. Breasting their hatred and his own terror, he struck out frantically for a shore he never reckoned to gain.

He stepped between Ciddey and Dro, therefore between the whole ghost crowd and Dro. As he did so, Myal slung the musical instrument off his shoulder and clutched it in his hands, digging his own nails into the wood of the two necks. Ciddey checked instantly, and the rest of them behind her.

He shook the instrument at her—his hands were shaking anyway—and she recoiled.

"Remember what you told me," Myal said. His voice shook too. He wondered if his legs would give way.

Ciddey smiled. The smile showed only her lower teeth, and suddenly her eyes seemed to melt into black sockets.

"I remember, betrayer," she hissed. "I told you about my milk tooth and how my father thrust it into the wood to replace a piece of ivory that had fallen out. I remember."

"The tooth's your psychic link," said Myal. He stammered a little. He was now so cold he could barely feel what he held. The instrument might slip through his grasp, evade it as the pebble had. He must not let it. "If I destroy the tooth, you can't stay here. Can you?"

"No," she said softly, still smiling.

"I'll do it," he said.

"Oh," she said, "great ghost-killer." Then she laughed, except there was no sound. Out of her open mouth flew instead a silver blade, which landed on the paved street by Myal's boots and flopped there. It was his turn to recoil. Ciddey held out her left hand, and stream water dripped from it, trickled, gushed. The water poured around the landed fish, which was whirled up in it. Ciddey held the water there like a silver shawl, and the fish spiraled in the water. "You'll destroy the tooth, will you?" she said. "First you have to dig it out of the wood with your knife. Or do you have a knife? Perhaps you can borrow Parl Dro's. The knife he used to pick the locks of my house on the night he killed Cilny. But then," said Ciddey, twirling the water and the fish in bizarre loops and coils, "but then, I forgot. Even before that, you have to find out which of the pieces of ivory *is* my baby tooth. They're all so smooth now, and so yellowed. They all look the same. Don't they, *minstrel*?"

Myal stared at her, then at the instrument. Of course it was true. All those tiny clips of bone—he had never even counted how many—

Ciddey flung her shawl of water over him. He jerked aside at the vivid sting of its wetness, while the tail of the fish, completely palpable, horrible, thrashed his cheek. Then the crowd of dead things was pushing by, a single pulsing entity. He was smothered, trodden down, kicked, panicking and yelling, and then abruptly, thrusting through, surfacing, denying their force could affect him.

He struck bodies, cloaks, mail and hair out of his way. He had somehow a bright and detailed image of himself, as if a mirror were hung up in the air—a lunatic, teeth snarling, irises encircled by white, and he was sprinting. He wondered what he was doing, and before he had the answer he had already reached the end of the street where the overlaid roofs tumbled down across each other's backs. Or seemed to. Where, in fact, the bare hillside dropped off into the night. His arms were out, throwing something violently away. It seemed to be himself he was throwing, but then a weight was gone, and he was left behind it. A sharp cry of loss broke from him. But then the cry was covered by what seemed to him the most awful noise he had ever heard.

Flung into space, falling fast toward impact and death, the musical instrument screamed.

It was a shrill tearing scream, slender, fearsomely melodious, composed of many notes sounded all together and without pause. Its very soul seemed crying. It had been cobbled together, a drunkard's jest. It had come to life slowly as the boy Myal began stupidly, improbably, to play it. It had grown a spirit as a child grew length of bone and breadth of skin. It had grown life. It had belonged to Myal, and now he had killed it, and as it tore down the nothing of the atmosphere toward destruction, it shrieked to him. He knew it was only the air rushing up through the stops of the reed. He knew that. It made no difference.

He stood upright, but moaning ceaselessly, as if he had been hurt. He had. He did not even think to look back, to watch Ciddey Soban crouching in terror, tensed for the crash and the splintering which would shatter the linking tooth along with everything else. Myal had forgotten her, forgotten Tulotef, and Parl Dro. He merely wanted the scream to end, wanted the instrument's agony of fear to end in the quickness of the death blow.

Then the scream cut off, and Myal, spreading out his hands as if to fly, nearly pitched off the hillside in the instrument's wake.

It was Ciddey's mocking voice which brought him out of wherever it was his emotions had taken him, her voice crisp as the sound of a coin ringing on the street.

"You could never do anything right, Myal Lemyal, could you? Not even *that*."

Then he realized, too stunned to be glad or afraid, that he had not heard the impact after all of wood on stone. So he peered into the abyss, and saw, no longer than his thumbnail, the instrument suspended, caught by its frayed sling. From the bracket of the inn sign, streets below. For a moment his reason was outraged, for the inn, its sign, the bracket, were as insubstantial as the rest of Tulotef. Then he recalled the stunted little tree which had appeared where the inn had been in the morning. It was the *tree* which had arrested the instrument's fall. He could almost make it out, now he knew.

And behind him Ciddey, her link to living death unbroken, was saying to Parl Dro, just as Myal once had: "Lend me your knife. I can kill you with it."

CHAPTER THIRTEEN

Parl Dro stood and looked at the ghost girl, at her sad and evil and lovely face. He was aware the ultimate moments had arrived, inevitable as if they had been making love together, not hate. He had already braced himself. Despite the procrastination he had offered Myal, Dro had known this event was unavoidable when he sat in Sable's hovel. Maybe he had known all along, as maybe he had known it all. He had used Ciddey inexcusably, not from a fastidious loyalty to his trade, but to cement his own damaged psyche. And so what came now was just enough, though not exactly the justice she craved.

Quietly, he took out the knife she had asked him for and handed it to her, the hilt toward her hand.

She accepted it doubtfully, however. Even the deadalive could know surprise, as they could know any state that suited their basic pretense of life.

"Thank you," she said. But then: "It will be nice to stab you with your own blade."

"Good."

"Where should I strike," she said, "to hurt you the most,

155

and leave you alive the longest? You see, I want Tulotef to have you, too."

He looked beyond her. To him, they were only a vague tumult, like mists boiling on the hill—archaic, stagnant ghosts. Their buildings were half-drawn in soft gray chalk against the sky. Beside the phantoms of the Ghyste, Ciddey looked very human. And Myal—he looked flesh and blood, kneeling on the hill's edge, the dark-gold hair, the patchwork showman's clothes, the pale face eaten alive with fright and personal trauma.

"Try for the guts," said Dro to Ciddey. "It might be messy. Twist the knife a little, and it will be messier. If you get it right, a man can last up to three quarters of an hour, puking blood most of the time."

He saw her drain whiter than her own whiteness and her eyelids flickered as if she were going to faint. She could kill, naturally, but the description had unnerved her.

"Maybe I will," she said, biting her lip. "As you die, you'll feel *their* claws. But you know what that feels like already, don't you, if the stories about your damaged leg are true? I heard that story about you when I was a child. The kiss of claws and teeth."

"Be careful," he said, "you're getting close to admitting your condition. You stole a lot of strength from Myal, and his inherent psychic powers let you become strong more quickly than is general. But to be a total success, you still have to believe you're wholly alive. At least, for a while. Until you've settled in. And then you'll find—"

"You're talking too much for a ghost-killer," said Ciddey. "I think I'll stop you."

Myal made an incoherent sound.

Dro glimpsed him jumping up, staggering, running toward Ciddey. Dro saw Myal's hand snatch at her arm from too far off, and the snatch passing through her sleeve, missing a grip on ghostly muscle or bone. Dro saw Myal's expression of utter non-comprehension as the knife thumped home in Dro's chest. Despite her words, as on the first occasion, she had aimed for the heart.

The blow had pushed Dro, but no more than that. He stood, and went on watching. He watched the red blood spread from the sides of the blade, which quivered like a metal leaf buried almost to the hilt in his flesh. He took a desolate interest in it. He had expected pain, but there was none. He had presumably gone beyond any new pain by now.

Ciddey had retreated. Amused she had backed into Myal, and they had each shifted aside to let the other pass. Dro half anticipated they would beg each other's pardon. Now she poised there, staring. Myal stared, too. This continued for about a minute. Finally, Dro reached up and pulled the knife out of his heart. It was thick with blood. Ciddey coughed out a toneless little screech. So far Myal was too shocked, or too astrally oriented, to throw up.

Behind them, the misty boilings of Ghyste Mortua were fading out. *They* had recognized, if no one else had, the futility of brute force. Maybe they had even figured out why.

Dro let the bloody knife drop to the ground. As if it were a cue, Ciddey dropped on her knees. She crawled to Dro over the street. She had forgotten the ghost duke and his retinue, just as they had let go of her and the guide she gave them back into partial reality. Her hands fastened on Dro's ankles and she shuddered.

"You're an avenging angel," she said. "Not a man, not a ghost-killer. An instrument of retribution."

"I thought that was you," he said.

"You're not even—not even—"

"Not even bleeding any more," he finished, helping her. "The mark of the knife will fade in a few days. Perhaps less."

"I must confess to you," she said. She cried tears on his black boots. "Will I go to hell?"

"There isn't a hell," he said.

He felt unbearably tired and shut his eyes. He hardly listened as she made her confession to his boots.

She told him in any case those things he had gradually come to understand when sorting his reactions to the leaning house, the room in the stone tower, the dark well, her devouring vindictiveness. Ciddey had not simply mourned her sister Cilny's death, she had caused it. They had had one of those frequent squabbles the village reported. It was hardly different from a hundred others, but its upshot was that Ciddey had pushed Cilny into the well. The younger sister had fallen across the rusty chain, clung to the bucket, but Ciddey had unwound the chain. It had been a long brevity of malice. When the struggles in the water had ended, Ciddey had

woken as if from a nightmare. She had been overcome by
horror. With a maniacal strength she had hauled up bucket
and chain once more, the lightweight dead weight draped
across it. Ciddey had flung her sister onto the paved yard.
She had tried to cudgel the water from her lungs. Weeping
more needless water on Cilny's drowned face, Ciddey had sat
and rocked her in her arms, confronting the ultimate loneliness of the deranged house of Soban. But in the night, Ciddey had carried and dragged her sister's corpse to the stream
below the mountain. Ciddey had woven her sister a wreath of
yellow asphodel, but Ciddey still hoped the current would
bear her sister away, out of sight and mind. Cilny, though,
being absolutely dead, sank heavily to the stream's floor.
Even the fierce spring wash of melted snow did not move
her. When the men found her and brought her back to Ciddey, Ciddey shaped her misery and her guilt into another
thing. She bore Cilny's ashes into the tower and worked
witchcraft with them. She brought Cilny back to her, and
cherished her dead as she had seldom done alive. Parl Dro
the exorcist had sundered that expiation, and all the murk in
Ciddey's soul transferred itself to him. But she had found out
now, Dro was not to be punished in her stead. Only Ciddey
remained vulnerable, to be her own scapegoat. She lay on the
street of Ghyste Mortua, and waited for nemesis.

But Parl Dro, who was not the somber angel of divine
wrath, did nothing, said nothing.

At last, Ciddey lifted her head. She experienced then a
strange wave of emptiness, or was it more a sense of
lightness, of the weight of Cilny slipping from her neck?

"I shall be punished," she said with curious dignity. "Will
you do it? What will happen?"

"You've been punished," Dro said. He looked at her wea-
rily. "You've punished yourself."

"I must suffer in hell," she said stubbornly. But a clear
hard tension was melting from her face, her body.

"There isn't any hell."

"Where shall I go, then?"

"Somewhere," he said. "Somewhere not here."

"Perhaps nowhere," she said. She stood up. Suddenly, everything she had fought for, or against, no longer mattered to
her. She did not see, but the tips of her pale fingers, her long

pale hair, became in that moment transparent again, as at her first manifestation.

"Somewhere," Dro repeated.

"Well," she said, "you'd know." She stared about her. An expression of uninterested incredulity crossed her face. "They've gone," she said. "The ghosts of the Ghyste."

"They're weak," Dro said. "They couldn't stand too much specific truth of this nature. Left to itself, any ghost will eventually die. It may take centuries, it still happens."

She stared at the luminous lightless revenant of the town. She even glanced at Myal.

"Why don't you," she said, "go down and take the instrument and get out the tooth and tread on it. I'll tell you which bit of ivory it is."

But Myal only flinched aside. He walked away and leaned his forehead against one of the ghostly houses. He did not intimate what he thought or meant to do, but he remained, perhaps unconsciously, in earshot.

"I *am* ready to go away," said Ciddey to Dro. "I'm tired. I want to. Why can't I just leave, without the tooth being smashed?"

"Once you've availed yourself of a link, the bond's established. You're tethered, till it's destroyed."

"You do it," she said imperiously.

He smiled. He looked old and very handsome. Like a sculpture of a man, not a man. The stain of blood on his shirt had disappeared into its blackness.

"I don't think so."

"I don't understand," she said. "And yet—"

"Please," he said, an elegant, cold plea for tactful silence, which she ignored.

"*You*," she said. Her eyes flamed with amazement and knowledge. "*Charlatan*."

"Not quite."

"*Impostor*."

"Very well."

"Damn you," she said, "how dared you—"

"How dared you?"

She shut her mouth. She smiled, her lips closed.

"I feel," she said, "serene. I don't care about you any more. I want to go to sleep. Or won't it be sleep? I don't mind. Let me go away. Please, Parl Dro."

"Myal," Dro said, not looking at him, "go and climb the tree and fetch the instrument."

Myal turned his head, trying to push it through the transparent wall, somehow not able to.

"Go to hell," Myal muttered.

"There isn't any hell," said Ciddey reflexively. She laughed. It was a girl's laughter. "Perhaps I'll find Cilny," she said. "She could punish me. And then we could be reconciled. Oh, I'm tired of being *here*. Can *I* get the instrument and break the link?"

"I don't know," Dro said.

"I hated you," she said. "How I hated you. My motive for coming back. But you."

"Please," he said again.

She shrugged.

"Oh," she said. She glanced again at Myal. "Him, I suppose. I thought you'd have to follow him into Tulotef," she said, "because you were in love with him."

"I am," said Dro, "in love with him. He's my son."

Three things happened in a neat and tasteful choreography. The girl widened her eyes, started to question in a gesture of hands rather than words; that was the first thing. Secondly, very, very slowly, Myal wrenched himself off the wall and began struggling toward them in a kind of brainless lurch. The third thing negated all previous actions. It was a sound. The sound of tearing cloth. The frayed sling, all that held the heavy musical instrument to the rough rods of the tree, parting.

The three incorporealities left on the ghost street were transfixed. A last, abbreviated dim wail, one single note, drifted up to them. Then the crash of wood on jagged rock, a wild twanging of wires, scuff of stones, dull dreadful bouncing, slamming, sliding. The soft little rush of shale, a sharp crack. The second crash, total. Feathers of silence came drifting down.

Ciddey spun like a cobweb, the skirts of her dress fanning out, forming insectile wings.

"I wanted it," she said. "I think I made it happen. I'm glad," she said. She wept, not the beads of the cold fish stream, only tears. "I want to—" she said. "I want to—"

The darkness spun like a wheel, spinning her away with it. Sometimes it *was* possible to comfort, to smooth the path.

The going through could be calm, even in some cases blissful, thankful.

But Dro stood and looked at the night, feeling only an intense and acrid shame, a rejection of everything he had ever done in the name of his so-called profession.

Automatically, not really meaning to, he put up his arm to block Myal's blow when it came flailing for his jaw. Automatically, Dro returned the blow, light as a cat. Myal sat down on the street, cursing him.

Though he dreaded it, Parl Dro now had his own confession to make.

"You can't, you couldn't be my rotten father. Unless you started very young. I suppose you could have. I was too scared to—there was never any opportunity—no, I was too scared. A carter's wife seduced me when I was twenty. *Twenty.* She was the first. I was grateful. You must have been at it when you were fourteen. Or less. And with a mature woman. That doesn't seem very salubrious. Did it with her and strolled—sorry, *hobbled*—off and left her. Left her with my drunken pig of a father—only he wasn't. No wonder he hated me. Whenever he thumped me, he was thumping you. I don't blame him. I'd like to smash your head in. *Father.* Traveling ghost-killer. Can do clever tricks with knives. You'll have to teach me that one. Padding, metal plate, fake blood. Or is it the knife that's the trick, the blade bends or something? You really will have to teach me, *Daddy.* You owe me something. If it's even true."

"It's true."

"Well I've only got your word for it. And either way, what's your word worth? I've lost the only thing that was any use," said Myal. "It's down the slope, in pieces."

"Where you originally tried to throw it to save me from Ciddey and Tulotef," said Dro. "I realized then, you'd have to be told."

"I don't want to hear anything else," Myal said.

"And, frankly, I don't want to tell you anything else," Dro answered.

"Great. We'll keep it that way."

Myal got up. His head bowed forward, eyes on the ground, he strode away, long fast strides that Dro's crippled leg should have some trouble competing with. And then Parl Dro was standing directly in front of him. Myal pulled up, eyes swimming.

"What—how did you manage that?"

"The same way I managed the knife. The same way I got from Sable's hovel in the forest to this hill in less than a minute."

"You tranced yourself, after all," said Myal. "You're here in the astral, just like I am."

"There's a low wall behind you. Sit on it."

Myal retreated a step, and the wall caught the backs of his knees. He sat, not entirely meaning to. "All right."

"Now," said Dro, "if you can keep quiet, I'll explain. Despite the fact I may not want to, and you may not want to hear."

Myal gripped his hands together, and stared at them trembling.

"Why do it then?"

Dro did not reply. He sat on the wall half a yard away and presently began to speak in a low still voice that did not hurry or slur a single word.

Parl Dro, from the age of seventeen a practicing exorcist, had turned forty when he walked into the wood below the mountain in the dusk, and found a woman with Silky's golden hair, a woman who *was* Silky, still alive and matured to an age that was just a few years less than his own. He had not loved her, but he had found her. And she, responding to some resonance of that finding, or to the simple hunger of her own sparse existence, had come to meet him on the inevitable road. The outcome might have been anything, a parting, or a continuance. But the outcome had not been permitted to create itself, it had been forced by the arrival of the showman with the drunkard's face and belly and the inappropriately stylish musician's hands. He had been away that night, bargaining for the unique musical instrument which that other drunkard, Soban, had offered him. The showman had meant to bed in a brothel, but in the end the price of drink, and the price of the instrument, had taken all his cash. With the prize in a leather sack, he careered home, all the while wondering if he had been a fool, to his wagon and his wife. And discovered someone had called in the night. "Come on, I don't care," the showman had said. Maybe in those moments, with the philosophical detachment of liquor, he did not. But sobering and caring caught him up. He climbed into the wagon then and selected a weapon. It was actually a meat cleaver. He got back on the horse and went after Parl Dro, up the mountain, tracking him by pure animal instinct born of hate. And when he reached Dro, the showman swung the cleaver with an unerring intuition, attacking the weakest point, Dro's crippled leg. The razor-like blade sheared straight through flesh, sinew and bone, as it was its job to do. The leg was severed just below the knee. Parl Dro did not know it, knew only agony. He fell away from his assailant, and in a sudden panic, the assailant let him go. He turned his horse and fled and soon enough had the wagon on the road again, driving back into the south country. The gold-haired woman, whom he had struck unconscious as his very first deed, before even going for the cleaver, regained her senses in that moving wagon. By then the blood and the weapon had been tidied. She assumed her man's vengeance had been visited on her alone, or had wished to assume so.

On the mountain, having rolled into the narrow channel, Parl Dro lay until his intelligence went out in pain and blood loss. And after awhile, he bled to death. Unequivocally. Completely. He was dead.

He had come to think, when he lived, that he understood almost all a man could learn of the foibles, motivations, methods and devices of the deadalive. How they were jealous of the living, returned for retribution, sucked energy from those who loved them—particularly kindred—hid their wounds usually from others and themselves, or, very occasionally flaunted those wounds to inspire terror and guilt. That rain did not moisten their garments, which were always those of the hour of their deaths. That they came by night, because the darkness aided in masking the flaws of their physical disguise, but also because their superstition made them chary, unless abnormally strong and self-assured, of the brilliancy of the sun. All those things he had known. They had been helpful. But most of all Tulotef had helped. Not only because it had been his goal on the day he died—Ghyste Mortua, that essential pilgrimage of so many ghost-killers, the ghost town of ghosts who pillaged mortals—but because, along with a motive for return, it had insured that he had previously learned certain disciplines. Believing the thesis that only in the astral form could a man enter the Ghyste safely, Parl Dro had set himself to acquire the skill of trance, and the subsequent psychic release of the spirit body out of his flesh. By the time he died on the mountain, he had been a master of the technique some months. And so the thing occurred which he, with all his understanding of the undead, would never have supposed possible.

A battle began, on some extra-physical plane that had to do with the world and with some other place beyond it. The battle was between the two entities into which Parl Dro had split. One entity was furious to live, to seek Tulotef and destroy it—now an ironical desire indeed. This entity, armed with its psychic disciplines, knew it could re-project itself into the world in a whole and perfect astral form, the most lifelike and undetectable ghost that had ever resisted its death. But the second entity had remained an exorcist, and this entity fought the first, trying to drive it away into that otherworld to which now it rightfully belonged.

If Tulotef had been the only drawing force that called him back into the world of flesh, it was likely Dro the killer of ghosts would have won that ultimate war against his own revenant. But, of course, there was the link, also. An irresistible link. Something that had belonged to him. But better than a bone or a glove, better than a tooth or a hank of shining hair. Much better. Much more enduring.

Probably at first she had convinced her brutish man that he was responsible. He would have turned to her now and then, as if to the beerskin or home cooking. Eventually, after her death, and as the child grew, the showman would have seen certain things. The light build which was hers, but the height which was neither hers nor his, the hair which was her color but a tone or so darker, the eyes which went sometimes black. The face, too, which by curious turns became piercingly good-looking. And the genius, which came out in music with a talent the showman had never possessed. Myal. Parl Dro's seed. Seed which had grown into an embryo, a child, a boy, a man. Something, nevertheless, which Dro had left behind in the mortal world. Myal, his son: the *link*.

On the plane where the two entities of Parl Dro fought each other, ghost-killer with ghost, there was no time. But in the world, time passed. And as it passed, so Myal, growing into adulthood, became a link which, more and more strongly, called Dro back to life. In the end, the deadalive Dro had won. Then the calling was reversed. He called to Myal blindly, seeing, if it could be described even as "seeing," only the link. Myal, who was psychic, and joined also by kinship, reacted to that tug, not knowing it. Still not knowing, he wandered back from the south, into those woods and over that mountain. He went by his father's decayed and crumbled bones, and naturally did not know that either. He wandered into the valley village and waited, unknowing, for Dro to win the final victory, and come back through the gate to apparent mortality. And Dro, galvanized by Myal's physical proximity, roused. In stasis, he was the same age as at the instant of death, thinking the events of twenty-six-odd years before had happened two or three days ago. Accordingly, he sought the wagon in the wood and failed to find it, and next he resumed his interrupted—how interrupted!—journey over the mountain.

By the time Parl Dro walked over that mountain, and toward the Soban house, he had become truly the King of Swords, Death, an emperor of ghosts. And of deception. The deception of others, and of himself.

For here was a deadalive who had been trained to know every pitfall, every giveaway. He made no mistakes. The rain dampened his garments. The dust brushed over him. He paused to eat and drink. He slept. He made love. He could bleed, and scar, briefly. Though not, of course, die. He walked in agony on a whole but ruined leg, remembering only the ghoul on the bridge—yet, covering such distances—climbing rocks, and *trees*. . . . He would lever up the catch on a door rather than pass straight through it. And often, though maybe not always when there was no one by, he would manifest in daylight. He could even fool his fellow dead.

A true ghost, he had fed from the living. And he had fed from Myal. He, not Ciddey, had begun to drain him. Though presently, Dro had unconsciously recognized what he did, and tried to pull away, just as Myal, as frantically, kept after him, attracted, making excuses, snared. And then, from some well of discipline and will inside himself, Parl Dro had managed yet another feat to which ghosts did not generally apply themselves. He had ceased drawing off Myal's living energy. Dro had begun to build a facsimile of that force instead, as

with all his other extraordinary powers, *within himself*—a
self-perpetuating flame. Even in retrospect, he was uncertain
when this transfer had taken place. Like all ghosts, he obscured, at that time, his own nature from himself, as he had
obscured his need of Myal before.

Myal was psychic. He had inherited that from Dro. It had
enabled him to follow Dro, when Dro had truly meant not to
be followed, or seen, or found. Myal had other qualities
besides, qualities Dro had never had time to accumulate, and
which Myal had not had the scope to develop. Myal, who
could be more stupid and ineffectual than Dro could ever
have dreamed of being, live or dead, had some glimmering
sequin inside him, brain or spirit, that had sprung out of the
soul of the world. Dro could not destroy that, whatever he
might now feel about his own condition.

Some part of him had known always, of course, that he
was dead. However powerful and extraordinary, still dead.
He had gone after the ghost of Cilny with an unlawful dedication—the dedication of one who slays the plague victim in
terror of perceiving the same symptoms in himself. The
Ghyste had been a similar fixation. But now that he had confronted himself and what he was, now he knew he should be
going, as Ciddey had gone at last so blithely and with such
grace, shaming him—now he could not leave the world. For
the link must be metamorphosed—burnt, crushed, dissolved.
Dro's link was Myal. In order to be free of his own imitation
life, Dro would have to take Myal's life. Dro would have to
kill his son. It was Myal's apparent death that had first
shocked Dro back toward self-realization. He could not face
that death again, not even with his own as the result of it.

One alternative remained. To get away from Myal now
and forever. For though he did not need to feed from Myal's
life force anymore, Myal was the motive, the rope that bound
Dro to the world, or rather to which his deadaliveness clung.
Cinnabar had grasped that fact, while not even comprehend-
ing it. Unless she had. She had thrust Myal into Ghyste
Mortua as Dro's safeguard, his mental anchor in the midst of
supernatural chaos. Yes, probably she had known it was a
demon lover in her bed sixteen seas deep. Just as she had
known he saw Myal's mother in her. Just as she had known it
all.

Myal was sitting now, staring at the earth. He cried easily, not necessarily a flaw, though plainly he himself categorized it as such, for he attempted to hide the crying from the weird dead father at the other end of the wall.

Dro had never loved anything, anyone. Not even Silky, who had only been a part of himself, as Myal was.

"I'm sorry about the instrument," said Dro matter-of-factly.

"Damn the instrument." Myal cried harder, for he had loved the instrument. He tried harder to hide the crying. He tapped the wall with his long neurasthenic fingers. It did not look like a wall any more. It was a ridge of the bare hill. The building and the blank yellow lamps were gone, and the bells and wheels and hammers and songs. Maybe they had exorcised Tulotef after all. Just talked it away by a recital of cruel truths.

"I'm sorry about everything," said Dro.

"But you told me."

"It's your right to know."

"But not my right to hope anything good will ever happen."

Parl Dro picked up a flint. Idly, but swiftly, on the ridge he scratched his name. Backwards.

"And now I'm going," Dro said.

"Don't—" Myal looked up. He was afraid.

"Get out of this place, and walk back to Sable's hovel. You'll find it easy to locate, because you're there, in the flesh. By tomorrow, you should be able to get into your body again. You're stronger than you think."

"I'm not as strong as *you* think. You think I can take all this and stay sane. Well I can't. Where will you go?"

"Just somewhere to wait."

"What for?"

"To die. In my entirety. Ghosts do die. I've learned that from Tulotef. Particularly with no incentive, it could be quite quick."

"Why not," said Myal flippantly, "wait till *I* die. The link would break then, wouldn't it?"

"You might live a long time. I hope you do. But I've got no right to be here. Think about my problem. I spent my life killing for a cause. I can't refuse to kill myself for the same ethics."

"You bastard."

"Try to learn some new dialogue," Dro said.

"More like yours," Myal sneered.

"Preferably more like your own."

Myal started to say something, but the sentence stayed in his mouth, because Parl Dro, handsome Death, the King of Swords, had vanished between one breath and another.

For ten minutes, Myal charged about the hill. He shouted to Dro, or against Dro. Then he stumbled and slid, and when he came to rest hard against a spike of rock that seemed to have been set there purposely to impale him, he felt something snap under his shoulder. He looked, and found he was lying on the shambles of the broken instrument.

"You learn to play this, you ugly cretinous little rat," Myal's father had affectionately said to him—but not his father, after all, had he not always suspected? "I killed a man because of that. I killed him good and dead."

Myal supposed it *was* because of the instrument. Because of his father—his *un*father—being away to buy the instrument, Dro had slept with Myal's mother.

"I killed him good and dead."

Myal held the broken sound box in his arms, and wept in the dead black country of the night.

CHAPTER ONE

———•◦◦•———

As the sun westered, it dyed the great branched candelabra of the trees. Trunks and boughs were steeped in patches of yellow-amber. The leaves were shining saffron, a prophecy of the autumn, no longer so far away, for the westering of the day allegorized the westering of the whole year. The end of summer was an arid scent, like the dust along the road.

Myal walked at a rhythmic pace. At each step, the bag on his shoulder jounced. There was a stringed instrument in the bag, nothing odd about it, a battered vintage guitar he had diced for in a ramshackle village, and, to his surprise, won. He had been thinking about the best way to portion and cut the body when he could find a twin for it and how to cut the twin too. Then there was a suitable reed to come by, and all the carpentry which these things would require, to fix them in place. He did not make the plans quite lightly, either, for remembrance of their forerunner still gnawed at his heart. It always would. He had buried the bits of wood and wire on the hill of Tulotef. The first grave made there for centuries. Certainly, the first grave to be mourned.

But grief did not have to jeopardize other emotions. The awareness of being inside real flesh made him secure, just as

practicing the trance state of astral release exhilarated him.
There had also been some luck in the past month. Gambler's
luck and minstrel's luck. Even luck with a girl in a lowland
cottage, a girl who wanted only a day and night, and not all
his days and nights thereafter. Maybe the old woman in the
hovel had blessed him. He had given her a present of three of
the silver pegs from the dead instrument, since she had cared
for him so well during his . . . absence. She had also sewn
his shirt together where she had cut it previously, searching
for the drug that tranced him. Actually, her name was not
Sable. That was just the scrawl on the door which related to
a former tenant. Parl Dro had not been right about everything. This notion had cheered Myal, as, with a droll cunning, he set out on his quest. He had been cheered as well by
the memory of how he had achieved success before, against
greater odds, when he was delirious with a fever and the on-
slaughts of two greedy deadalive.

He was not apprehensive now, not even desperate anymore. Merely determined, like any heir to a fortune, to claim
his birthright. Dro had only one thing of worth to offer Myal,
and that was the acid elixir of his own company; his erudi-
tion, his harsh judgment, the razors of his tongue and his
mind. Myal had grown up in a beast pit, and the earth had
gone on looking that way. He was tired of it. He needed a
new vantage. He understood Dro could give Myal his own
self, or show him where his self was to be found. He did not
intend Dro, who had sown him accidentally, and abandoned
him in death, to get away with it. Myal had acquired the
trick from women he had had trouble with, maybe. But it
was still a valid trick, and he had the knack of it: blackmail.

For the rest, he knew Dro would no longer vampirize him.
Dro was independent to a fault, and had learned to fuel himself, like some volcanic fire, once ignited. Myal's other role,
as Parl Dro's reason for life—or reminder to live—Myal accepted gladly, and with amused pride and a desire to please.
It was fine, even funny, that till Myal died, Dro would not.
Improvising on the humor, Myal had now one mad recurring
vision, which tended to make him giddy with laughter. It con-
cerned himself at fifty-five or so, and Parl Dro, his father,
still looking the age of the hour of his death, some fifteen
years younger than his son. Or perhaps Dro would age now,
logically, a master of all life's disguises.

"It's easy to follow you," Myal had said to Parl, beside the fire in the ruined fortress, as the night shook with fever. "You leave a kind of shadow behind you. I can't see it with my eyes, but I know it's there. I can find you simple as breath."

It was admittedly a little harder to trace a man permanently in astral form, once he had decided to remain mostly invisible. Yet here and there, the beacon sent out its ray, the habit of corporeality proving too much for even Parl Dro's fortitude. And meantime, the link itself was the best guideline in the world. And what would Myal say when he caught him up? It was still difficult to be sure how to get around someone like Dro. Though, of course, now he believed he could do it. Somehow.

The sun burned in the black flames of poplars.

The high sky was only a clear luminous parasol. No cloud. Not even a bird. Not yet even a star.

But the unseen shading was vivid. It had led him over a hunchbacked hill, off the road, down a meandering track and farther into the trees. The light began to go suddenly, like water running through the fingers.

"You're a magician," Myal could say to Parl. "You can kid anyone you're only a man, but you can walk through walls. You're invulnerable to death by blade or rope or poison or any other normal agency. You could get in a king's vault and steal anything you felt like. And you want to throw all that away? As a professional thief, I resent that."

And he could say to him, "I never had a father. I had a thing with a leather strap in its hands."

And he could say to him, "You knew I'd come after you, like before. Stop making grand gestures and face facts. All right, you're guilty about the others you sent off. But you're determined to survive however you possibly can."

The fulvous leaves softened into dark greens and umbers, and the branching stems were cool as ash. The glade was empty, or appeared to be.

Myal stopped, and looked at it, swallowing his heart as usual, glancing casually at a particular vacant area between two trunks.

"Well," said Myal, his voice light and carrying, with an exquisite diction.

In the area between the trees, the unseen shadow emerged, dim and formless.

"I said," said Myal, "well."

And then he fired sheer will across the glade, the psychic's instrument of intent and survival. It hit the place between the trees, bound and held, and hauled. And Parl Dro evolved, filled in by velvet blacks, till the paler sculpture of the face was firmly marked between ebony mantle and raven's hair.

Parl Dro looked at Myal with slight anger and mild interest. His disapproval was almost comic in that instant, his foreboding beauty almost touching; his despair, if he did despair, was hidden.

And Myal laughed at him, and Myal looked himself beautiful and ruthless as a gold angel fallen straight from the setting sun. Just like the prince he had always really known he was.

"Well," drawled Myal for the third time, knowing now what to say. "*Fancy* meeting you."

Presenting MICHAEL MOORCOCK
in DAW editions

The Elric Novels

The Runestaff Novels

The Michael Kane Novels

The Oswald Bastable Novels

Other Titles

If you wish to order these titles,

please see the coupon in

the back of this book.

Attention:

DAW COLLECTORS

Many readers of DAW Books have written requesting information on early titles and book numbers to assist in the collection of DAW editions since the first of our titles appeared in April 1972.

We have prepared a several-pages-long list of all DAW titles, giving their sequence numbers, original and current order numbers, and ISBN numbers. And of course the authors and book titles, as well as reissues.

If you think that this list will be of help, you may have a copy by writing to the address below and enclosing fifty cents in stamps or coins to cover the handling and postage costs.

DAW BOOKS, INC. Dept. C
1633 Broadway
New York, N.Y. 10019

DAW presents TANITH LEE